IN DARKNESS IT WAITS

DASH DUVALL

Publisher, Copyright, and Additional Information

In Darkness It Waits by Dash Duvall
www.dashlduvall.com
Copyright © 2023 by Dash Duvall

ISBN- 979-8-856-36835-1

Editing by Erin Young

Cover design and interior design by Rafael Andres

1. TOLONGO ISLE

Halloween Eve, 11:59 p.m.

Jett Jefferies lay awake near midnight, reluctant to admit he was bored with life. Seventh grade was effortless—his tests a snooze-fest. Little league was five months away; his New Orleans Otters had come in second last spring due to his pitching. Katarine—the girl he liked—had moved to Sea Island in August, and his closest friend, Wells, had gone to visit his sick grandmother in Charleston for the week. So, Jett had nothing to look forward to, and that was his one complaint.

Slumped against his pillow, hands interlocked behind his head, Jett fantasized about more interesting lives: a Wild West gunslinger on horseback robbing trains; an astronaut in a rocket ship launching into space; a gladiator wielding a sword in the Roman Colosseum, triumphantly standing over a lion. What amazing lives!

But, Jett realized, tomorrow is Halloween.

A strange sound interrupted his thoughts. He strained to listen over the pattering rain. *Squeakkk, squeakkk.*

A few days ago, a FedEx truck had crumpled his Schwinn bicycle which he left by the mailbox. *Squeakkk, squeakkk* the broken axels groaned as Jett had wheeled the bike to the curb. But now the sound was clear. And it sounded, well, *clean.*

Jett sprung from bed and peered into the muddy backyard. There it was. His forest-green Schwinn bicycle, sitting in perfect condition under the watery moonlight. *Squeakkk, squeakkk.* The bike wheeled closer.

Jett smiled and raced into the hall, bursting with joy as he recalled the wonderful days riding to Wells's and to Katarine's, to little league practice, to toilet-paper mean Mr. Lasenberry's oak trees. His Schwinn was his escape, his avoidance of tedious days. Now it was back, gleaming and pristine.

Jett threw open the back door in the kitchen, letting in cold wind and mist. *Squeakkk, squeakkk.* The bike moved a foot nearer as Jett grabbed an olive-green slicker off the coat rack, tossed the hood over his curly, jet-black hair, and darted into the backyard. A shimmering fog formed.

Squeakkk, squeakkk. His bike inched forward as rain tapped Jett's hood and his bare feet muddied in the sodden lawn. *But how is the bike pedaling by itself?* he thought suddenly. *And, wait, fixed bikes don't squeak?* The fog thickened.

"Huh?" Jett gasped.

Belligerent, red eyes appeared in the darkness, just beyond the fog.

"Gotsta get home," came a voice. "Fulfilled my duty... yes, yes..."

Jett squinted into the fog as a depraved scarecrow stepped through. Its face was sinewy, hair made of rotten straw, and it wore a sagging, pointed cap on its head.

"Fulfilled my duty, yes, yes," the scarecrow chattered, smiling at Jett without teeth, its mouth an endless shadow. "The Umbras owe me, yes indeed. The greedy, nasty Umbras... gotsta get home. After all... this... time." The scarecrow caressed a brilliant, midnight-blue gem hanging from its neck in a gold chain. "Gotsta get home," it repeated. "And *you're* gonna help me do it, aren't you, Jett?" It held out a trenchant, skeletal hand.

Squeakkk, squeakkk. The bike headed right to Jett's feet.

"See!" the scarecrow cackled. "Good as can be. Go on, Jett... take a seat..."

Entranced, Jett reached for the handle. A light flicked on in the kitchen. Jett spun.

His dad was standing at the kitchen door in his tattered Emory University shirt. His dad gazed outside and adjusted his browline eyeglasses. "What are you doing, Jett?" he called out. "Get back inside!"

His mom sidled his dad and tied her lavender robe.

"I'll be back," the scarecrow crooned, fading into the fog. "I'll get you soon. Yes, yes." The fog evaporated with the scarecrow's image.

"*Jett*," his mom repeated. "Listen to your father *this instant*!"

Jett ran into the kitchen. His bare feet muddied the tile. "Mom, Dad, a scarecrow mended my bike! I, uhh—"

His mom drew his hood. "What are you talking about, honey?"

He pointed into the backyard. "My bike's fixed."

"Your bike? Impossible." His dad squared his glasses and surveyed backyard, murky with rain. "I don't see anything except wet grass and our old patio furniture."

Jett turned and a breath escaped him. Indeed, his Schwinn was gone. "I swear it was... I was talking to..."

"A scarecrow?" his dad said, uneasy.

"A man lured you outside?" his mom confirmed.

Jett nodded, embarrassed.

"Alton. Your gun."

His dad raced into the master bedroom and returned with a revolver. "Jett, show me where."

His mom clicked on a flashlight and, together, the Jefferies family filtered out the kitchen.

"Hello," his dad shouted. "If anyone's here, know that I have a gun!"

"Shhhhh," his mom whispered. "Listen..."

Jett paused. Wind rustled the leaves. Raindrops clicked in puddles. Branches groaned.

"Where was the man dressed like a scarecrow?" his dad probed.

Jett motioned toward the hedges.

"I have a gun!"

"*Alton.*"

The flashlight wobbled as the trio crept over. His mom shined the flashlight across the lawn. His dad crouched at the hedges and ran a finger through a tire tread. He glanced up, startled. "Sheryl, call 9-1-1."

***

Halloween, 1:11 a.m.

The detective who strutted into the Jefferies's home an hour later had highly alert eyes and long maroon hair. She wore a camel trenchcoat, a plaid trilby hat, and leather gloves. She clapped loudly after entering. "Yes, who are you?" She leered at Jett, ignoring his parents and the meek policemen who arrived earlier.

"The, erm, victim?" Jett said, ill at ease.

"I'll be the judge of that." The detective set her gloves in her hat and passed them a cop. "I'm Detective Dreyfus. Twenty pragmatic years solving cases for N.O.P.D., thank you very much." She flashed her credentials, stored them in her trenchcoat. "Am I to understand that you saw a *scarecrow*... on Halloween?" she asked lazily.

"The scarecrow talked to me." Jett nodded. "Fixed my bike."

Detective Dreyfus ferreted out a notebook, clicked a pen. "You enjoyed riding this Schwinn, I presume? Did you cause trouble on it with your friends?"

"No...?"

"Jett's an honor student at Isidore Newman," his mom cut in.

"Cunning people get away with more things." Detective Dreyfus scrawled something on the notepad. "Intelligence creates bravado, and conceit. Jett, is this the first time you've met a ghost?"

"A *scarecrow*. And *yes*."

"Who fixes bicycles in his spare time, right. I wonder what trade-school scarecrows attend... are you on prescription medication? Do you have psychological issues I ought to know of?"

"I saw the tire tracks with my own eyes," his dad asserted.

"Yet the Schwinn has disappeared. Do I understand that?"

"Yes." Jett was angry and confused.

Detective Dreyfus ticked something off her notepad. "What did this scarecrow say to you?"

"It wanted to get home. It completed a task for someone named Umbra, I think."

"Umbra?" Detective Dreyfus tapped the pen against her chin. "Doesn't ring a bell. Did it mention where 'home' is or what the 'task' was?"

Jett shook his head. "Everything was abrupt."

Detective Dreyfus huffed and marched into the kitchen. The group followed.

"Stay where you are," she ordered at the edge of the room, then wandered about, suspiciously opening drawers, the pantry, the refrigerator, studying the tile littered with muddy footprints, muttering. "I see. I see... Yes. I think I'm getting it." She stopped at the light fixture. "Mr. Jefferies, which switch did you use when you ran in here?"

"It's Dr. And the second one."

Detective Dreyfus hit the switch. The kitchen light flicked off, then on. "Fitting. And what brought you into the kitchen?"

Jett's dad crossed his arms. "The howling wind. The door banging against the counter. Paternal instinct? Take your pick."

Detective Dreyfus continued prowling. The expression on her face was like she was gaining some marvelous insight. "So, Jett, you happened to wake when you heard your bike outside... in the wind and rain... or—" she ripped open the fridge, pulled out a Fiadone cheesecake with a slice missing, and flopped it on the island "—were you down here... sneaking an unauthorized piece of dessert?"

"I didn't eat that!"

"Prove it. Because I say this 'scarecrow' is a hoax to cover up the real crime!"

"I ate the cheesecake," Jett's dad professed, catching a glare from his mom.

Detective Dreyfus tutted, crossed something else off. "One confession down. One to go."

"Detective, aren't you being... rather disparaging?" said his mom.

"Mrs. Jefferies, you do realize it's Halloween? Surely you understand that children, the mischievous little imaginators they are, love pranks." Detective Dreyfus opened the back door and swaggered into yard, now with slack rain. The group tailed her. Jett snagged the flashlight.

Detective Dreyfus crouched by the hedges and examined the tire tracks. She ran a finger through the mud, licked it spotless. "Hmm. Yes." She stood. "You might be wondering why I brought you out here," she said to no one in particular.

"Uhh, not really," said his dad.

"A bicycle was here tonight, I agree. It's possible a costumed scarecrow was riding it. But there was no abduction, nor any verifiable threat made against the boy's life. Perhaps trespassing was committed, but the real crime is wasting my time." Detective Dreyfus reached for her gloves and hat from the cop and impatiently shoved them on. "Dr. and Mrs. Jefferies—please have better sense than falling for an imaginative plot next time you phone N.O.P.D. Now, *goodnight*!"

In utter astonishment, Jett watched Detective Dreyfus storm out the side gate and disappear into the night.

"Well, she's half-right," an officer chuckled. "Her coming here was a waste of time."

"So you believe me?" Jett asked.

"Err, sure, kid," muttered the officer. "Sure."

***

Halloween, 9:33 a.m.

The morning arrived with sparkling sunshine. Seated at the kitchen table, Jett brooded over the implausibility of the scarecrow's presence.

"How 'bout last night?" his dad laughed, biting a biscuit drizzled with andouille gravy. "You can be quite convincing, buddy. Maybe you should be a lawyer, like granddad? I can see you stalking around a courtroom, swaying juries."

Jett gulped his orange juice. He wasn't fond of the notion.

"Or how about a movie director?" his mom said, peppering eggs Benedict. "Your mind works the right way for that."

Jett didn't mind this. Still, he rolled his eyes.

Breep. Breep. Breep. His dad's cell. His dad groaned at the caller ID. "The office on a Saturday..." He answered. "Beulah, yes, how are you—yes—well *fine*, put the patient through if it's that pressing. Hi, this is Dr. Jefferies." His dad's face morphed into fascination. "*Really*? Wait, so you're not sick?—Well, certainly. Text me your address—great—be there in an hour." His dad hung up, beaming. "You won't believe it. That was Cooper LaBeouf."

***

Halloween, 10:11 a.m.

Jett didn't like Cooper LaBeouf's house from the moment he laid eyes on it. It was an old, entresol townhome with peeling, peach paint and mildewed paneling. Cooper opened the door as the Jefferies parked and waved at them stiffly.

Cooper's face was haggard, hair matted and grey, and he wore a bedraggled pilot jacket.

Jett followed his parents up the sidewalk.

"Happy Halloween." Cooper coughed. "So, Jett, I take it you know who I am?"

"That paranormal investigator who goes on talk shows."

Cooper gave a weak grin and ushered the Jefferies in. "Last night must have been alarming. Hearing about a scarecrow on the police scanner certainly caught my attention." Cooper looked to Jett with a grim expression. "Your encounter wasn't your overactive imagination, nor was it isolated. The encounters have been happening to children in New Orleans on Halloween for centuries."

Jett's heart thumped against his ribs. The group went into the living room.

"I've spent my career studying supernatural phenomena, collaborating with police precincts and even federal agencies on their most obscure cases." Cooper gestured the Jefferies to an old sofa. He took a holey recliner. "After thirty-odd years of investigations, one and only case of mine remains unsolved. It's more than a case really. It's a paradox. And it involves that scarecrow who approached you last night."

Jett shivered.

"I called your dad because New Orleans has a curse, Jett. I called because I need proof that I haven't gone crazy." Cooper scooted forward in the recliner. "What we're dealing with: is a monster." He pointed at a rubber-banded file struggling to hold its contents on the coffee table. "Inside you'll find declassified paperwork from the F.B.I. and N.O.P.D., plus hundreds of photocopies from City Archives. Decades of bizarre disappearances in New Orleans on Halloween. All marked unsolved or christened 'NO CRIME'."

Jett reached for the folder. His mom yanked his hand back.

"Of course, there are mothballs in the history," Cooper went on, glancing out the window as if searching for something. "Only seventy percent of cases mention the scarecrow, and only forty reference the shimmering fog. For a long time, I thought everything was coincidence... until I found this." Cooper grabbed a dingy book off the end-table. Its wooden cover was etched with stars, half-moons, and a pirate ship, though no title or author. "A professor at Tulane put me in touch with a collector of French colonial artifacts out in Lafayette. Bartered ten thousand to get it. But once I read its contents, I knew *this* was the key." He laid the book on his lap. "Jett, the shimmering fog you were immersed in last night is the very shimmering fog that floated out of a cave on Tolongo Isle in 1723."

"With all due respect," Jett's mom said, "I think you've grown obsessive and myopic, Mr. LaBeouf. I mean, come on."

"Do you get out much?" added his dad. "Come to think of it, it's been a while since I've seen you on TV."

Cooper smiled. It was polite, unoffended. "I understand your position. Allow me to read a few pages?"

"Please," said Jett.

"I believe this book was compiled by a harbormaster who worked with the French Navy in the Caribbean." Cooper opened the volume. "From the beginning then."

"*October. 1723. Dusk.*

I've been asked by Captain Stowe to write this letter, as neither he nor I know how much time we have left. Six days ago, we navigated our two-mast galleon, The Houngan, to Tolongo Isle in hopes of finding a hideaway. On paper, Tolongo Isle seemed to be as good as any...

Devoid of life, Tolongo is a horseshoed bay with walls of unclimbable rock. The water eddies here without wind, shimmering fog floats at night, and the bodies—the bodies of several of our crew—float around our ship, touched by not a thing. What disturbs Captain Stowe and I most, however, is the towering slit in the rock face: a cave so dark it appears to be a black hole from the cosmos... and it is there I fear we must go.

A curtain of impenetrable fog formed at the inlet's opening the moment we pulled in, and a torrential, swirling tide grew, trapping us. The first day stranded at Tolongo, three of our crew members lowered into a lifeboat and fought their way ashore. We watched from the deck as the three slipped inside the cave. Hours we waited, but the crew never resurfaced, nor did we see a light or hear a scream.

The following morning, four more took the spare lifeboat ashore, only for the same to occur. Thereafter, we five remaining elected to bide our time with the food and water in our stores. The fourth day came, all rainless. Our salt pork, hard tack, and turnips were depleted, and we were growing wary. The rum and wine went on the fifth day, and a madness settled in us. On the sixth morning Captain Stowe and I woke to a quiet pother, so we set out to find our crew. Caution rose in us as we roved the hull, for we heard sounds of faint chewing, grindings, and mastication. What Captain Stowe and I stumbled upon was a *scene of desperation: John Teach and Bonny Scouse had taken Ben Blackthorn's head by cleaver and were gnawing his tendons. Their wild eyes snapped up at us, faces riddled in hives. Our pistols drew quickly.*

Bound and chained, Captain Stowe and I forced the cannibals off the plank. It is their bodies which now float around The Houngan.

So here Captain Stowe and I sit, throats desiccated, stomachs shaking, enticed by a musket to the brain. We have done what we can to endure this wretched place.

Whoever finds this letter, please know what happened to us, and know that I wish you not the same. Captain Stowe and I have loaded our pistols and are heading for the cave. If there is indeed something within, it is patient and wicked and awaits in the dark.

Bartholomew Reneer, First Mate

Cooper turned the page and continued reading aloud.

Admiral Dublier of the French Navy cleared his throat after reading Bartholomew Reneer's letter to his crew. Standing with him were twenty naval officers adorned in light blue, brass-button uniforms. A head taller than everyone, Admiral Dublier took in their prudent faces as he surveyed the room.

'A ruse,' said his commander. 'These pirates only mean to run a rig!'

An ensign stepped closer. 'The pirates have abandoned their ship and left their loot. How is it a ruse with corpses floating in the water too?'

'The pirates merely did a respectable job,' barked the commander. 'Admiral, we know Captain Stowe—he's clever, sure, shifty as a lynx—but he's no match for us. We can take whatever's in that cave, be it pirates or a fickle beast.'

'Kervens,' Admiral Dublier called out.

Their guide, rushed forward and removed his red felt cap. 'Sir?'

'What d'you think?'

Kervens fidgeted. 'Tell you the truth, I dunno, sir. Never heard anything like it.'

'But you have been to Tolongo Isle?'

'No, no. These are cursed waters. This is a vile, evil place.'

The commander lunged at Kervens. 'Why didn't you say—'

Admiral Dublier gestured him away. 'Kervens, do you mean to tell me there really is something... incorporeal in that cave?'

Kervens began to perspire. 'All I know is dark priests have been coming to these waters for centuries... practicing...'

'Damn your blood, guide!' the commander yelled. 'You're just trying to absolve yourself of your duties.'

'Commander!' Admiral Dublier frowned. 'Kervens, Captain Stowe left your port last week?'

'I showed you our journal entries. And you spoke with the harbormaster. Captain Stowe said he was heading between Tortuga and the West Indies.'

Admiral Dublier paced a minute then paused to speak. 'Men, here's what I gather: the most likely scenario is that Captain Stowe and his crew had a second ship stashed here at Tolongo. They took their most-valued treasures and forged this note in attempt to get us off their tail.' He motioned through a small window into the night. 'In the hour we've been here, we've seen no shimmering fog nor any rogue tide. As for the bodies, the men could've been mutineers or captives.' He snatched his flintlock pistol off Captain Stowe's desk and stuffed it in his medallioned belt. 'I say we look in the cave. Odds are Captain Stowe and his crew are halfway back to La Nouvelle-Orléans by now... where Admiral de Champlain awaits.'

'And if you're wrong?' asked the ensign.

'We're armed. Ready the rowboats.' Admiral Dublier proceeded onto the Houngan's deck.

Outside, the night was starless and cool without wind, making the black water look like a pit. He strolled lankily under limp sails past the rail-cannons *and glanced at his warship in the open sea, then he studied the abandoned lifeboats ashore and instinctively fingered his compass. It had stopped working. The cave weighed on him heavily. It was so black it seemed to swallow other shadows around it.*

In silence, Admiral Dublier led the rowboats across the water. Bayonets drawn, torches lit, his platoon breeched shore and trotted over. Inexplicable heat and the fetid stench of spoiled meat emanated from the cave's opening.

'Surely the den of a beast,' whispered an ensign.

The commander scrunched his nose. ''d explain the reek.'

'But not the heat,' Admiral Dublier countered and loosened his collar. 'Men, comport yourselves. If Captain Stowe is inside, we want him alive. The people of La Nouvelle-Orléans deserve to see this pirate hang.'

Single file, the platoon filtered in. Their torchlights flickered against the steep, slimy walls as they entered a tall chamber with a swallet in the ground and dripping offshoots jutting out. An ensign inched to the swallet. 'What d'you make of it, Admiral?'

Admiral Dublier stepped forward and dropped in his torch. The flame tumbled over on itself and disappeared into the shadows without sound. He cocked an eyebrow as the commander sidled him.

'Tunnels could go on forever. Don't think it's wise for us to wander. We could burn The Houngan and leave.'

'Well, your attitude's changed,' said Admiral Dublier. 'The darkness getting to you, or is it the reek?'

'Neither,' the commander muttered. 'Nor is it the heat. But there is something about this place. Don't you agree?'

Admiral Dublier huddled the platoon. 'Pair off and investigate the offshoots, but return in a few minutes. No lingering. And for God's sake don't fire at each other.' The platoon ominously nodded. 'Kervens and I will remain and keep watch.'

The platoon broke and rambled down different passageways, leaving Admiral Dublier and Kervens. 'There is something,' Admiral Dublier admitted. 'Something I can't put my finger on.'

Kervens tugged Admiral Dublier's uniform. 'We should leave. Mystic priests... awaken things.'

A faint buzzing. Kervens swatted at it beyond their torchlight. It was like a fly. Admiral Dublier did the same and the humming faded, but the temperature rose dramatically. Admiral Dublier rubbed his neck. His forehead beaded. 'Kervens, what's happening?'

The heat became suffocating. Admiral Dublier eyed the cool twilight air behind them. The fresh breeze seemed so tempting, so right in the moonlight.

Before his mind could say otherwise, he took off. Kervens did the same. The duo practically flew outside. 'This is hysteria!' Admiral Dublier grumped, clutching his knees. 'A fever from bad fish likely.' He gazed at his warship in the open ocean. Only he couldn't. A thick wall of shimmering fog had risen and now hung like a curtain against the bay. A tide in the water grew.

Don't. A voice in his mind. DON'T turn around.

Admiral Dublier could feel something watching him. It was the presence he had sensed on The Houngan deck. Fog crawled over his boots. His gut wrenched as Admiral Dublier realized that Bartholomew Reneer's letter had been real, a genuine warning from his enemy. Admiral Dublier glanced at Kervens through the corner of his eye. Kervens looked back with eyes wide as Admiral Dublier set a hand on his flintlock pistol and turned.

His soul nearly fled his body. A scarecrow with belligerent red eyes, wearing a billowing black duster, stood gaping. It had a sinewy, depraved face and hair of rotten straw. On its head was a sagging, pointed cap. 'At last,' it crooned, 'someone I can fit into.' With a clawing stroke, it snatched Admiral Dublier by the neck and—SNAP—Admiral Dublier collapsed. Kervens jumped in the water and swam desperately toward—'"

"Mr. LaBeouf!" shouted Jett's mom. "That's enough."

"No keep going!" Jett leapt from the sofa.

Cooper glanced at Mr. and Mrs. Jefferies.

"Maybe just the synopsis?" said Jett's dad, looking pale.

"Well," said Cooper. "The Gulog got dressed in Admiral Dublier's skin and clothes and—"

"In his *skin*?" gasped Jett.

"The Gulog is rather tall, you see. It needed Admiral Dublier's *height*."

"The Gulog's its name?"

"What the Tortugais call the monster," said Cooper. "Anyway, it rolled Admiral Dublier's body into the black duster then into the water. By the time the platoon exited the cave, Tolongo Isle was like it had been, no fog or tide or anything strange. And the Gulog—disguised as Admiral Dublier—ordered the platoon back to the warship and to burn The Houngan on the way."

"What about Kervens?" Jett asked.

"Found swimming toward The Houngan. When the platoon reached him, Kervens was shivering and refused to get in the same boat as 'Admiral Dublier.' Presumably fearing for his life, he remained quiet. And *that's* how the Gulog came to New Orleans three-hundred years ago."

Jett tried to wrap his mind around this. Had he really encountered the Gulog last night? "Why doesn't the F.B.I. go find it?" he demanded.

"Because the F.B.I. doesn't believe in crackpot stories and hornswoggling," his mom blurted. "I admit, Cooper, you had me for a moment. And I truly was afraid last night. But let's be serious... you have an uncorroborated old book and a litany of misappropriated cold cases. What you're suggesting is illogical."

This made sense to Jett. His tension receded a bit.

"Under common thought, yes," Cooper said.

Jett's dad retrieved his phone and searched something. "I don't see Tolongo Isle on the map."

"That's because it was wiped away by a hurricane," Cooper explained. "You'd have to visit the Caribbean Institute for Meteorology and Hydrology to discover it."

"But where did the Gulog come from?" Jett asked. "And why does it stay in New Orleans?"

"*That—*" Cooper started to his feet "—is exactly the information I'm after." He moved to a shelf of intricate electronics: digital recording devices, motion-activated cameras, tri-field meters, EMF detectors, and infrared thermometers. "I'd like to confect a surveillance grid at your home tonight and stick around to survey it. This may seem odd, but at worst, it's a useless precaution."

"You want to spend the night at our home?" asked his mom.

"I'd be in a van on the street. And I won't be sleeping."

"It's an invasion of privacy."

"Have you done this before?" said his dad.

"Well, no. Only because I've never met a child who escaped the monster."

"You really believe the Gulog is after me?" Jett said, aggrieved.

Cooper nodded but did not elaborate.

"*Why*? I didn't do anything!"

"I don't know why the Gulog chooses specific children or how it slinks about unseen."

"Shouldn't we leave town?" Jett said.

Cooper rubbed his chin. "I suppose."

"We could go to my folks' at Lake Pontchartrain?" recommended his dad.

"Please!" said Jett. "I'd like to see Thanksgiving."

"Sheryl?"

"If Jett would feel safer, I don't see the harm," she replied.

His dad rubbed his palms together, glanced at Jett. "Which means we can stop at Marie's."

"Marie's?" Cooper gave a small chuckle.

"This diner off Highway 190. They make the best muddled cherry pie. One bite and you think you've gone to heaven and died."

2. HORN HOUSE

Halloween, 4:44 p.m.

Jett and his parents reached the Lake Pontchartrain causeway and found the northbound bridge shut down. "What sort of idiot crashes a boat into a drawbridge?" his dad grumbled, reversing their car in a sea of honking horns. "If you're rich enough to have a tri-deck, you're rich enough to hire a captain." He eyed Jett. "Sorry, bud. No muddled cherry pie. How about we stop off and buy candy? We'll stay in tonight. Everything will be fine."

A rock dropped in Jett's stomach. "I hope you're right."

***

Halloween, 8:55 p.m.

Nighttime. Famed paranormal investigator Cooper LaBeouf was monitoring the Jefferies's home in his surveillance van, via the electronic equipment he placed throughout the house and taped against the walls. Jett's dad had verified every door and window was locked and his mom had tucked him in. Now lying in bed, Jett was chewing a caramel square and watching TV when the disembodied voices came.

"Welp, there's no one here, *Bob*," said one. "Ain't a person or creature up this way in years. 'cept maybe those we don't want to know about."

"Still, *Buzz*, a walkthrough made sense," the other voice chimed. "Especially with them fishy accounts we've been hearing."

Clear as day, the voices were coming from under Jett's bed. He muted the TV and perched on the end of the mattress, alert and cautious.

"A hasty idea and a sensible one are altogether different," said Buzz.

"Dad!" Jett yelped, kneading his comforter. "COME QUICK."

Heavy footfalls in the hall. His dad threw open the door. "What? What is it?"

"Someone's under my bed!"

His dad flipped on the light. "I think you're scaring yourself, buddy." He knelt by Jett's bed, pulled up the curtain, and peered under.

"Well?" Jett scrambled over.

"Whoa!"

"What?"

"There's an animal down here."

"WHAT?"

"Yeah... a great big dust bunny." His dad popped up with a grin.

"Not funny!"

His dad stood. "There's nothing down there. Enjoy that caramel and try to rest. You're safe."

"But—"

"Night, Jett." His dad flipped off the lights and wandered away.

Jett looked out the window. No shimmering fog in the backyard. No bike.

"Face the facts, Bob," Buzz's voice came.

"*You* face the facts, Buzz!"

Baffled, Jett slipped off his bed to the floor.

"Last time I listen to you."

"Oh, and I guess you're the captain of bright ideas?" Bob said back.

Jett clasped the bed curtain and, with a brave gulp lifted it. Old toy boxes were crammed underneath, nothing else. But the voices kept on.

"We've an enormous job to do," Buzz said. "And you want to burrow all the way out to Redroot Forest... I'm beginning to think you've become a doddery twit."

"What better place to hide?" said Bob. "*Think*, Buzz. THINK. How many know about this ole house anyway?"

The voices weren't scary like the Gulog's had been. Bob and Buzz sounded thickheaded, comical even. Jett dragged the nearest boxes out from his bed. Still, he saw nothing unordinary.

"Well... maybe your idea does hold ground..." Buzz granted.

"Aha! So you admit it. Course it does. COURSE. IT. DOES."

"Yet, there's no one in this rundown house."

"Yes, but what of the footprints?"

"Mostly *ours*. Who knows how long the others have been here. Redroot Forest is a preservation. This house has been off-limits for ages."

Bob huffed.

"Back to Focal City then. Plenty to do with Cape Nautic this morning, plenty to do."

A door closed.

Fascinated and not feeling particularly frightened, Jett army-crawled under his box spring. He wriggled deeper and deeper and pushed toys out of the way as a slender light beam grew in the dark. He crawled farther. The light brightened and brightened and—"Ouch!" He banged his head against something. "Ouch," he repeated, rubbing it. Something wooden had appeared in front of him. Jett rolled over and reached up. His box spring had *vanished*. Panicking, he flipped onto his stomach and tried reversing out, but his heels rammed into a barrier. "Whaaaa—" He kicked it. No luck. A mystic wall had formed behind him. He wanted to cry out, to plead for help, but he was smothered by a wave of claustrophobia and fear. Had he fallen asleep in front of the TV? He must be slumped in his bed in front of the TV, the caramel melting in his hand. He stood, carefully, reached toward the light, and felt... a doorknob? Cold as ice. With a twist, it opened, and Jett found himself staring down a hall in a vast house with dusty oak floors. Through the mullioned windows, he saw a sprawling forest made of reddish sequoias under a violet sky with *two* suns—one scarlet, one pale white. Jett tip-toed out of the closet into this new world, listening for Bob or Buzz.

Silence.

Jett roamed around. The house was abandoned, clearly. There was no furniture on the ground floor except an antique, teak dresser in the parlor. Jett sifted through. The top three drawers were empty. The bottom one, however, held a slinged battlehorn made of dense, black bone and etched in a language he'd never seen. The battlehorn's ends were bronze encrusted, as if a relic of a war. Jett placed it over his shoulder. But where was he? A terrible thought came: was he in the Gulog's house? A sudden, great desire to distance himself came. He rushed out the door into a nippy day, trying to compose himself.

Far beyond Redroot Forest, to his left, stood colossal, frosty mountains which soared into the clouds. To his right, Redroot Forest extended down into serene countryside. Directly before him were two holes of upturned dirt leading into the woods. *Bob and Buzz really did burrow here,* Jett thought, marveling.

"Alright then," he said to himself. "If the Gulog wants me, it'll have to come find me." Jett trundled down the hill toward the burrow holes but at the last second stopped, and surveyed around, feeling eyes on him. He saw nothing, so kept on, and entered the thick undergrowth below the Redroot canopy. For hours, Jett wandered, pausing at every twig snapping or rustling of leaves while following the burrow trails—which navigated effortlessly around thickets and trunks before stopping at a babbling creek where, apparently, Bob and Buzz had jumped out and walked over a bridge before recommencing their burrowing on the other side.

From the bridge's apex, Jett peered into the crystal water, which calmed him. Water always did. Vampire crabs beetled about in the sand. Bioluminescent seahorses played, bubbles bursting from their long snouts. He watched the creatures in peace and absorbed the hollow sound of the running creek. It was a state of tranquility.

A red dot formed in the distance. A rapid hum. Across Redroot, a man-sized, flying red mantis zoomed over. The red mantis's wings flapped incredibly fast. It swooped over the creek, clutching a net, dipped the net in, and scooped out a band of seahorses.

"*Stop that,*" Jett shouted. "Leave them be!" The seahorses thrashed in the net, shot black ink from their snouts. "You heard me. Let them go!"

As if just noticing Jett, the red mantis glared ferally at him, huffed, and flew back from where it came. Feeling helpless, Jett sighed and pressed on, soon encountering more miraculous sights: plump, pink, giggling fairies hovering over upright blue tortoises chasing them from the ground; cream-colored monkeys bouncing on the stomach of a furry, snoring hippo; and a golden tufted kitsune with nine tails playing with her litter at the end of a rainbow! Like the red mantis, every creature acknowledged Jett with scowls, though none ran away or charged him.

When Jett emerged from Redroot Forest, the suns were much higher. He watched them crisscross like a strain of DNA and temporarily combine into a single, magnificent tangerine orb.

The burrow trails ended a stone's throw from the forest edge, near a dilapidated road littered with crunchy leaves. A pair of tire tracks cut across the pavement. *Bob and Buzz must have driven back to society*, Jett guessed. And if not, well, at least he had found a sign of civilization, although a sign of great disrepair it was—absolutely quiet and full of cracks and divots.

It seemed there really were no visitors in Redroot Forest. But if that were true, why was Horn House built so deep within it? And why had it been abandoned? Jett wondered these thoughts, among many others, feeling scared, unsure, and a tinge of excitement, as he stepped onto the crackly leaves and began his walk to who knows where.

3. Recher Town

Jett walked down the barren road in this strange land, his thoughts uninterrupted as no bird nor critter nor vehicle came by, only the breeze playing with the leaves. How had that inexplicable boundary opened under his bed? Why had it opened—*Is the Gulog luring me somewhere? How am I supposed to get back?* Around a bend, Jett came upon a chrome-orange scooter leaning against its kickstand. A battery was installed below the seat and on the front was a cargo tub stuffed with magazines, newspapers, and letters out for delivery. Jett eyed *The Focal City Fanzine.* The newspaper had a headline: GOVERNOR

NESS WIDENS REACH OF THE ORDINANCE OF ORDER.

"'Oi!'"

Jett jumped.

A pudgy boy his age with wide, rosy cheeks and a mop of tousled, marigold hair was marching out of Redroot Forest.

"You scared me." Jett held a hand over his heart.

"I meant to," the boy roared. "You've got *some* nerve trying to steal my Silver Pigeon."

"I wasn't trying to *steal* it." Jett rubbed his arm, nervous. "I was... admiring it."

"*Right*... like you wasn't trying to steal my Silver Pigeon."

"I promise," Jett stressed. "I'm lost. I don't know where I am."

The boy nodded at the battlehorn. "Steal *that* as well?"

"I've never stolen a thing! I found this battlehorn in a house."

"You found the battlehorn in a house, yet you didn't steal it?" The boy scowled. "I've right mind to turn you in." A bolt of curiosity struck the boy, it seemed. "Wait, *what* house? We're way outside town."

Jett gestured back down the road. "Deep in Redroot."

"No one lives in Redroot but Odin Stine. And I just came from his treehouse."

"You're not *listening*. I don't know how I'm here and I don't know where here is. I walked out of a closet in an abandoned house. I'm frightened. Can you help me?"

Whatever the boy expected Jett to say, it wasn't this. "Hold up." The boy held his a hand out. "Are you trying to say you're a Boundary Walker?"

"Huh?"

The boy squinted. "*Where* in Pararealm did you boundary walk from?"

"*Pararealm*?" The word exploded in Jett's mind. "I came from Earth."

"*E-e-earth*?" The boy lurched back. "You boundary walked from Earth?"

"I don't know what that means!"

"A Boundary Walker can cross dimensions. Like slipping between wrinkles in space."

Time stood still. Jett contemplated. "That's what I did?"

The boy scrutinized him. "Why were you trying to visit Pararealm?"

"I wasn't trying to do anything," Jett avowed. "One minute, I was protecting myself from the Gulog. The next I was—"

The boy recoiled. "The Gulog? The murdering lich!"

"You know of it?"

"'Course. Ripped Ruth Schrödinger apart years ago. At least, that's what I believe." The boy shook his head, downcast. "Ruth was the most revered Quantum Manipulator in Pararealm. One of the most beloved people in history."

"I had no idea..." Jett's eyes traced the leaves on the road, his brain churned. "That's not the story in New Orleans."

"Batty name, New Orleans." The boy grinned. "Tell me everything."

And so Jett apprised the boy of his Schwinn bicycle mysteriously squeaking through his backyard, shrouded in shimmering fog, of the portal opening under his bed, and of tracking Bob and Buzz from Horn House.

The boy was left speechless at first. "So, Bob and Buzz Fuzz were out snooping in Redroot?" He began worriedly rubbing his chin. "And there's an abandoned house out there? Interesting."

"I don't understand—who are they?"

"The police. The whole Fuzz family belongs to the department and gets suspicious about anything new to them. Power-driven, they are, always obeying Governor Ness." The battery on the Silver Pigeon glowed green. "Hop on and I'll explain. I'm Horace, by the way." He stuck out his hand. "Horace Hane."

Jett shook it and boarded the Silver Pigeon. Horace twisted the grip and the boys took off at impossible speed.

Quick as they started, they came to a stop, and Jett's stomach went flopping. He wobbled to a lawn as Horace dismounted. "Runs on helioki-netic energy." He motioned to the battery then the suns. "All our abilities are powered by them."

Jett gawked. "Abilities?"

"Yes, *abilities*."

"Ahh, morning, Horace." A mellifluous voice rose up the hillside. "Who's your friend?"

Outside the country chateau stood a willowy man with long, silver-streaked black hair, cir-cular eyewear, and an eggplant-purple topcoat. Horace grabbed a furled-up copy of *The Focal City Fanzine* and told Jett, "Powerful electrosorcerer, he is. Likes his news prompt." Horace raced up the exterior stone steps, exchanged niceties with the man, then ventured back down with him.

"Jett, is it?" the man asked. "Horace tells me you're from Earth. Been many, many ages since an Earthling visited our world. It was not pleasant."

"I didn't mean to come," Jett insisted. "I don't know what happened."

"So said the last Earthling. Alas, he made it back, or maybe I'm misremembering..."

"I'm not sure what to do," Horace admitted. "With The Ordinance of Order and everything."

"Why didn't you just... go back?" the man asked Jett.

"I couldn't! I was trapped."

"So you had no intention of visiting Pararealm, and quickly became stranded. Something foul is at work."

"What should I do with him?" Horace reiterated.

The man cast his eyes at the horizon. "Best to keep quiet and not stir up things in Recher Town. Earthling, you're in competent hands with Horace. No need to be terrified, not yet anyway. Horace, m'boy, I'll have a think and come back to you."

Horace nodded, appreciative. "Why don't you stop by the cottage tonight?"

"Can't. I've been summoned to Focal City for business." The man glanced at Jett. His thoughts were unreadable. "Best of luck, Earthling. I hope you find your way back quickly."

The battery of the Silver Pigeon dinged.

"Well... see ya, Mr. Thorne," said Horace.

Jett again climbed aboard, and, with a twist, he and Horace zoomed away.

"Should I be worried?" Jett asked at the next stop, once recovered from the temporary nausea.

"You're fine." Horace dismissively waved.

"You trust Mr. Thorne?

"We're family friends. Sorta."

Jett wasn't sure about this. Still, he asked, "So, if everyone has an ability, what's yours?"

"This!" Horace's voice boomed inside Jett's head. "I can communicate via mindlink. Pops is telepathic too. Mom is a mimicist—she can augment her body to resemble stuff around her, like a chameleon. My sister, Honor—" Horace rolled his eyes "—is a mimicist as well."

***

Many stops later, the morning deliveries concluded, Recher Town came into view as Horace slowed the Silver Pigeon at the crest of a hill. Picket-fenced cottages and homely shops lined the quaint streets, along with a lone commercial building and a squat educational institution. Recher Town was idyllic.

Horace slowly navigated to the bottom of the hill then onto a trail behind a row of cottages.

"Who's that, Horace?"

Jett glanced up. A boy was leaning from the second-story window of an elegant cottage. He had pebble-colored skin, seafoam-green eyes, and long incisors.

"Do I know you?" Horace called back.

The boy turned up his chin. "Horace. Who is that?"

"My cousin. Not much more I can say, Xander. Way above your paygrade."

"I didn't know you have a cousin?"

"Well, you don't know everything, do you?"

Horace wended toward his cottage.

Jett jumped off the Silver Pigeon with him. "And Xander is... ?"

"Annoying. Mom says he looks up to me, which doesn't make sense. I mean. We're the same height." Horace walked the Silver Pigeon through his back gate. "Plus Xander has these kitsunes which I'm allergic to. I can't go inside the Dhampir's without sneezing my head off."

The boys entered the Hane's residence. "Mom, I'm back!"

"Horace," she hollered, deep in the cottage. "You don't have to scream every time you return." Mrs. Hane entered the sitting room and stopped at Jett's sight. "Oh. You didn't say you brought company, Horace. Who's this?" Mrs. Hane's hair was lighter than Horace's marigold. It was golden-white. Her face was fair and shrewd, which reminded Jett of a swan.

"This is Jett." Horace presented him. "We met near Odin Stine's."

"Okay..." Mrs. Hane said expectingly.

"Jett wandered out of Redroot. Actually, Jett wandered much farther than that."

"Right..."

"Jett boundary walked... from Earth."

Mrs. Hane went ghost white. She rushed over and clasped Jett. "Oh dear. Are you hurt?"

Jett debriefed Mrs. Hane the same way he had Horace. But this gave him no more reassurance. "But *why* must I stay hidden?" he asked. "What is The Ordinance of Order?"

Mrs. Hane gave him a glum stare. "I'm afraid you arrived in Pararealm at a dismal stretch. Governor Ness has been broadening his authority via the decrement of unjust laws. The most severe—The Ordinance of Order—stipulates that every citizen must receive an audit, which measures one's ability in each paranormal field."

"Why is that wrong?"

"On the surface, it's not. But there are rumors that people are disappearing if they show a propensity for reality warping." Mrs. Hane cast her eyes away, distraught. "Many are trying to grasp the underlying agenda behind Governor Ness's actions. And to make matters worse, war, it seems, is imminent."

Jett swallowed dryly. "War, you say?"

"Between Governor Ness and the Iconoclasts," Horace explained.

"The Iconoclasts are spreaders of discord," said Mrs. Hane. "They are the rebels who refused the audit." She turned to Horace. "This morning the Iconoclasts set a Poltergeist Bomb off in Cape Nautic—"

Horace was shocked. "It wasn't in the paper?"

"Will be tomorrow," Mrs. Hane said. "Every headline. Pop informed me via mindlink. Fifty poltergeists unleashed near the seaport." A shadow crossed her face. "Though that's nothing compared to what the Iconoclasts did to make their name."

Jett looked from Horace to Mrs. Hane.

"The Iconoclasts kidnapped a girl, Riley Schrödinger, the daughter of Ruth, the Quantum Manipulator I told you about," Horace said. "It was their first open act of mutiny."

"What happened?" Jett pressed.

"No one knows except those responsible." Mrs. Hane's brushed a tear away. "Riley lived alone with her father, Reese, after Ruth died. She was taken one night when their home was set ablaze. Reese funded a private campaign to find her, outside the Intelligence Service's investigation. But no trace of Riley ever came. And no ransom demand was ever made." Mrs. Hane exhaled. "The Schrödingers were a powerful, respected family, plagued by tragedy. No family should have to endure what they have."

"How do you know the Iconoclasts were responsible?" Jett asked.

"A note arrived at *The Focal City Fanzine*, bragging about the kidnapping with nonpublic detail. Ever since, the Fuzz and the Intelligence Service have attempted to find the Iconoclast stronghold with no avail."

"What do we do about Jett?" Horace urged.

Mrs. Hane took a minute to ruminate then extended her hand. "Yours, dear." Jett placed his hand in hers. Mrs. Hane closed her eyes, and, gradually, a mark appeared in the center of his palm: a gray circle with three intercrossing lines. "This designates that you're audited, but it's only a mimic." She held up her palm, displaying the true mark, then looked to Horace. "This won't pass more than an eye test. A temporary measure at best."

"What about his ability?"

Mrs. Hane focused on Jett. "Astral projection. Tough to identify, tougher still to prove. Jett, you're my nephew from Cape Nautic, an Astral Projector. Harlow, my husband, sent you here after the Poltergeist Bomb this morning. Your mother and father are arriving tonight. Remember that." She glanced at Horace. "Visit Ms. Gibbons. She can unveil this battlehorn's mysteries and perhaps provide more guidance on Jett's arrival."

"It's safe?" Jett verified, memorizing his alias.

Mrs. Hane gave a comforting smile. "The Fuzz mostly stick to Focal City and Enopolis. And with the scene at Cape Nautic, you shouldn't have any problem."

"Man, and I thought today was gonna be a bore." Horace trotted toward the front door. Jett thanked Mrs. Hane and followed.

From a bowl on the foyer table, Horace snatched two tear-slips. "Vouchers," he explained. "Most travel between towns via teleportation pod, though Pop isn't wild about it."

"So, he works for the Intelligence Service?" Jett asked as they strolled through the front picket fence. "Aren't you worried about his safety in Cape Nautic?"

"Poltergeists are pesky but not dangerous," Horace said. "Besides, the I.S. will delegate the dirty work to the Fuzz."

"Can you speak with him right now via mindlink?"

Horace frowned. "Only if Pop initiates it. Takes loads of training to transmit messages far away. Besides, I'm sure he's busy." Horace gestured to the squat educational institution. "That's where Sooth Institute comes in. This satellite campus, anyway."

"You aren't in school?"

Horace blushed. "I, uhhh, got suspended for a few weeks."

Jett stared at Horace, prompting him to continue.

"Well, it wasn't my fault," Horace averred. "Mom made me this ostrich-egg salad and limburger cheese sandwich for lunch. And I, well, farted in the cafeteria. The whole room evacuated because the faculty thought I set off a stink grenade." Horace pushed Jett in a coltish way. "*It's not funny*. I can't continue my para-academic training until next trimester, so I'm stuck delivering mail every day."

Jett held in a laugh as the boys came to the sole commercial tower in Recher Town. A lit-up sign with dancing letters read: PSYMART. The boys ventured to the fifth floor. In the rear corner, a placard: TELEPORTATION NETWORK hung above a portly PsyMart employee wearing a navy vest. The employee was fast asleep and drooling onto his chest.

"Oi, Jasper." Horace poked him. "Jasper. We need a ride."

Jasper wrestled awake and accepted the vouchers. "Where to, Horace?"

"Round trip to Dowse Town."

Jasper punched a couple buttons on the intricate control panel aside him. "I know you from somewhere?" he asked Jett as the machine computed.

Jett gave a meager grin. "Ever visited Cape Nautic?"

Jasper sniffed. "Not in a while."

"Maybe you saw him in Focal City. Maybe you never saw him at all. Who cares?" griped Horace. "We've all been everywhere. Can we go, Jasper? We're in a rush."

"Hold your horses, eh." Jasper yanked a lever on the console. The console beeped and spit out a plume of smoke as Jasper fell back asleep.

Horace led Jett into a circular teleportation pod furnished with a curvy ivory sofa. They sat. The door closed. A vivid, silver flash filled the room. Horace rose. "Alright then." He headed for the door.

Jett was taken aback. "Wait, we're here already?"

Horace chuckled. "Yeah. And you ain't seen nothing yet..."

4. DOWSE TOWN

Jett followed Horace out of the teleportation pod into Dowse Town's PsyMart then descended into the lobby. "Shouldn't have problems," Horace repeated his mom. "But Dowse Town isn't as friendly. So, leave the talking to me."

Jett adjusted the battlehorn over his shoulder. "No issues over here."

The door attendant wearing a black fez hat scrutinized coming and going customers, most of whom were dressed in linen kaftans with beaded, lapis jewelry. The attendant crossed his arms and cocked an eyebrow at the boys. "Business?"

"Who are you, the authority?" Horace groused.

"Don't test me boy."

"We're visiting Doris Gibbons," Horace said with haste.

"That right?" The attendant straightened.

"Yes... the psychometrist... can we go..." drawled Horace.

The attendant pursed his lips and motioned them on. Kaolin clay homes and bodegas nestled around Dowse Town's central, shallow, rectangular pond. Camels with rainbow rugs across their humps and herds of aardvarks meandered the streets with citizens. In the backdrop, sanddunes ran endlessly in every direction. The boys traipsed around the pond to Ms. Gibbons's and knocked on her door.

"Maybe she's not here?" Jett said after a long wait.

Horace knocked harder. The door squeaked and shifted back. "Ms. Gibbons?" Horace called through the cracked door. "Hello?" He turned to Jett. Jett shrugged. The boys went in.

"Ms. Gibbons?" Jett announced.

A sable jackal leapt off a sofa and growled. It bared its whetted teeth.

"Anpu, back!" Horace snapped. "Get back."

The jackal prowled over. Its golden collar jingled, yellow eyes affixed on them.

Horace prodded Jett. "Grab a lambstick."

Jett snatched a jar of dried lamb off a stone shelf. Horace took one and wagged it at Anpu. As if hypnotized, the jackal licked his lips and followed it with his eyes. "Go... *fetch*." Horace threw the lambstick down the hall. Anpu spun and pounced happily on the treat.

"Phew." Horace wiped his head and set down the jar. "Now. I bet Doris is out back."

The boys exited into an arid backyard full of olive and mastic trees.

"See her?" Horace asked, scanning around.

"Reckon she's up there?"

A long set of rail-less steps ascended up a monstrous sand dune.

"Why couldn't she have been drinking tea in the parlor?" Horace grumbled. "Come on." The boys began their climb, escalating at a good clip at first but tiring quickly in the heat. "*Had* to visit today. Had to be today." Horace panted midway up the steps.

A gust of wind kicked up sand at the top of the dune. Jett sidestepped a girdled lizard and squinted across the tan, tumultuous horizon. "Got to be her, right?"

Across the flat, four cream pillars stood at the corners of an open-air granite sanctuary. A lithe woman wearing silk spangled garments and crystal necklaces sat meditating. Her legs were crossed, palms raised.

The boys roved over.

"You arrive with... concern, unknown one," Ms. Gibbons muttered, not opening an eye. "And Horace... you appear before me... inconvenienced."

Horace scowled. "Why're you up here?"

"It is easiest to listen in isolation."

"Your door's unlocked, you know."

"I encourage intruders. Anyone Anju deems unworthy is not okay by me."

"But you just—"

Jett nudged Horace's ribs. Horace quieted.

Ms. Gibbons opened her eyes, which were black as coal, and studied Jett. "You're lost. But from where?"

Jett started to answer.

"No." Ms. Gibbons rose and set a hand on Jett's shoulder. A mild current zapped through him and, in his mind, he saw a whirl of memories as if he was reliving his life. Ms. Gibbons removed her hand and the current stopped. A troubled look clouded her kind face. "An Earthling fleeing the Gulog... you must leave Pararealm at once."

"But how?" Jett asked, hoping for a clear answer.

"What lies ahead is unclear. As unclear as how you arrived."

"Is Jett a Boundary Walker?" Horace asked.

"I can't be certain, but I don't think..."

"That means—"

"Yes." Ms. Gibbons bowed in acknowledgement. "There is a Quantum Manipulator living in secret among us. And it is likely he or she was near Horn House when Jett crossed."

"Bob or Buzz Fuzz?" Horace laughed. "No chance."

"I mean someone else, Horace."

A chill ran down Jett's spine. He unslung the battlehorn and passed it to Ms. Gibbons. "I was told you could read this?"

The wind lifted as Ms. Gibbons took the artifact and again closed her eyes. She opened them after a moment. "This was forged eons ago. It is the horn of an ifrit, a prehistoric minotaur of huge proportion. The ifrit were evil...

necromantic beasts that roamed Pararealm near the time of the Spawning, then went extinct." She returned the ifrit horn to Jett. "This was deracinated during the Great War, between the Umbras and The King of Pararealm, long before democracy was instituted. Later, this battlehorn was gifted to Prince Icarus, the King's son and a tyrant."

The Umbras, Jett thought. "What happened? To the Umbras, I mean."

"'Tis a dark tale," Ms. Gibbons said. "The Umbras were ultimately defeated via a furtive ambush by a legendary warrior. The eldest Umbras were sentenced to death. The youngest were reeducated and granted amnesty... a grave mistake." Her eyes ran along the ornate battlehorn. "Thereafter, this laid deep in Focal City's caches, untouched, until it was stolen by a stockboy and traded for jewels. A gap in the reading lies from there, likely the merchant who bought it knew enough to cover the ifrit horn with neith—a fabric which prevents psychometric readings. Then... years after, it was bequeathed to a little girl... a young Uma Umbra."

The moisture dried in Jett's mouth. Horace grew pale.

"It found its way back to the Umbras?" Jett asked.

"So it seems."

"What should I do? Bury it here in the sand? Should I get rid of it?"

"For starters, no more touching it directly." Ms. Gibbons removed one of her silk scarves and wrapped the ifrit horn. "This will dampen psychometric readings, but, Horace, I suggest you buy neith. More importantly, ifrit were mischievous creatures. Their black magic can seep into you even if long deceased."

"Let's sell it!" Horace suggested. "Got to be worth a ton."

"I wouldn't," Ms. Gibbons warned. "Ifrit horns aren't items you come across every day. You may generate talk, which you don't want right now. Though—" she tapped her chin "—perhaps Galen the Chemizard has a benevolent use for it. And Galen is known for confidentiality."

"We didn't bring enough Teleportation Vouchers." Horace frowned.

"I didn't mean go alone. The Alluvial Lands are not a place two boys ought to travel unaccompanied." Ms. Gibbons refocused on Jett. "Another psychometrist can read you as I have. Allow me to overwrite your history and add astral ability into your memory." Again, a current zapped through him. His mind's eye whirled with fresh, disparate images.

"Thank you." Jett slung the scarved ifrit horn back on his shoulder. "You mentioned something... the Spawning?"

"Ah yes. Pararealm came into existence when the Karmabird split the orange sun and created heliokinetic energy. The Karmabird is our immortal guardian, who can see past, present, and future, and conduct psionic healing."

"That's why Odin lives in Redroot," said Horace. "Spends his days alone, searching the skies. The Karmabird is said to have a hundred-foot wingspan of gold, vermillion, and white feathers, though she prefers translucency most of the time."

"Right you are." Ms. Gibbons gestured toward the dune's edge. "Off you go, Earthling, may you not be destined to wander. Horace, give your family my best. Remember, I'll know whether you did when I see you next."

Horace grunted something which Jett didn't catch as they hurried across the sand.

5. THE ALLUVIAL LANDS

The refrigerator was open when Jett and Horace returned to Hane Cottage. A girl was humming behind it. Horace set a finger to his lips, excited, and snuck over.

"AHHHH!" The girl leapt from the fridge. "*Horace*! Don't scream in my head! It's incredibly—" she faltered at Jett's sight "—rude." The girl had braided, pearl-white hair, olive skin, and a button nose. She ambled past Horace, who was roaring with laughter. "You're the Earthling? I'm Honor."

Jett blushed. "Hi."

"You coping alright?"

"I suppose. We just got back from Dowse Town."

"Mom told me. The ifrit horn."

"So," said Horace. "Where's Lowell?"

Honor clenched her fists. "*That idiot*. I don't even want to think about him."

Horace grinned. "*Why*?"

"I caught him doing homework with another girl. Can you believe that?"

"No," said Jett.

"Of course!" Horace cackled. "Now, excuse us... Mom!"

"Horace. You of all people don't need to shout," Honor growled. "Oh, *wait*. You can't communicate with anyone not next to you."

"I'll be able to soon," Horace barked. "And when I can, I'll wake you up in the middle of the night! You'll never sleep."

"You wouldn't either then, stupid."

"Fine by me!"

"Well I'm installing a teleblocker. So good luck with that."

Mrs. Hane arrived in the kitchen. Horace and Honor's argument subdued, and the boys brought the group up to speed on Ms. Gibbons's reading.

"So, can you take us to Galen's?" Horace asked.

"Not this minute, Horace," answered his mom. "I have a shift at the regenerative clinic this evening. Besides, I'd rather have Pop go. Galen's a bit blinkered... and ornery. And the Alluvial Lands are primitive."

"Mom, *please*."

"She said no, Horace," Honor mocked.

"Mom, come on."

"No."

"Ughhh! You never let me do what I want," Horace groaned and floundered out of the kitchen to his room.

"Guess I'll check on him," Jett said after an awkward moment as Mrs. Hane gathered her things to leave. He found Horace stomping around his bedroom. Jett softly shut the door.

"They never let me do anything," Horace fumed. "Everything's on their time because their stuff is more important. I'm always shunted off to the side. I'm sick of it!"

Jett didn't know what to say, so he said nothing. Luckily, Horace brightened and raced into his closet, where he retrieved a magnifying glass and a rolled-up poster, then unraveled it on the floor, revealing a comprehensive map. Jett's examined all of Pararealm. There was Focal City (the capitol); Enopolis (the largest township); the dark and craggy High East; the Diluvian Sea and the Cape Nautic seaport bordering it; Redroot Forest, the snow-capped Sasqi Mountains and—

"—Galen's grotto. Right by this windmill in the Alluvial Lands." Horace surveyed the route through his magnifying glass.

"Should we be worried?" Jett asked.

"About what?"

"Didn't Ms. Gibbons say we need protection to visit the Alluvial Lands?"

"She's just being cautious."

"Well... what about Uma Umbra?"

Horace waved the idea away. "She fled to Umbra Castle years ago. No one's heard a peep."

Jett studied the depiction of a monstrous, black castle in the High East, far beyond the Sasqi Mountains. It gave him the chills. His eyes kept moving on the map. "Where's Horn House?"

"I told you," Horace stressed, "I had no clue Horn House existed. I don't know how Bob and Buzz did. Whoever built that manor in Redroot Forest did so in secret." Horace rose. "We can't get to the Alluvial Lands by teleportation voucher or road. Pop's air-rider will do, though.

Be quiet." Horace eased open the door, peeked into the sitting room, and motioned Jett on.

The boys bounded into the garage, where the Silver Pigeon was stored along with workbenches, mechanical wheels, disassembled engines, a jetpack, and a folded green sail on the wall. "Help me get this," Horace directed.

The boys heaved the sail off the wall and laid it on the ground. Horace unlatched the retractable wings and handlebar, then grabbed a conical device. "This is a windgun," Horace explained. "It generates an aerial current which propels the air-rider into the sky."

"We're *flying* to Galen's?"

"Sure," Horace said. "I've piloted the air-rider a million times. Now, just need the—"

"—garage opener."

Jett turned. Honor was leaning against the interior door, holding that very device, smiling. "Sneaking off, are we?"

"Oh, Honor," Horace said, feigning innocence. "Just taking Jett on a ride to, err, kill time."

"Yeah right—" she twirled her braided hair "—you're off to the Alluvial Lands."

Horace went red with ire.

"Well, don't you have a high opinion of yourself."

"Can't you just go away?"

"Ha. And what's your grand plan? Knock on Galen's grotto and convince him to buy the ifrit horn? Have you even determined its worth? Ifrit horns are ultra-valuable you realize." She began circling the boys. "Tell you what. Because I'm bored and can get extra credit for bringing cyanobacteria to my Botanical Regeneration course, I'll accompany you. But only to get a price quote. Agreed?"

Jett waited for Horace's lead. Horace said nothing.

"In return," Honor went on. "When we inevitably sell the ifrit horn for a higher price, I get a percentage of the profit."

"You cheat!"

Honor's eyes twinkled at Jett. "What do you think? The ifrit horn's yours anyway."

"Well—" Jett scratched his neck "—I don't see any harm in that."

"Great." Honor juggled the garage opener. "Now. I doubt we'll run into anything worse than a kappa, but if one is hungry or protective, we need to be prepared." She plucked aerosol cans from a shelf. "Toxispray for you two, and I get the windgun."

With a huff, Horace passed her the conical device, and Honor opened the garage. Jett and Horace carried the air-rider onto the lawn and fastened into the harness. Honor mounted the windgun to the back and strapped in. "Ready?" she asked.

"Ready," said Jett.

"Ready," Horace echoed.

The air-rider rocketed into the sky. Wind pulled Jett's cheeks and hair back as the air-rider ascended rapidly, buffeting this-a way and that-a way. "Amazing!" he cheered as the air-rider burst through a cloud. "No wonder the Karmabird sticks to the skies."

The air-rider straightened out and glided across the beatific horizon, curving around clouds and dipping below flocks of strige. Meanwhile, the ground below morphed into swampy wetland. The air warmed and a fishy stench rose.

"Kappas have spiked shellbacks the color of puke." Honor lowered toward the Alluvial Lands. "See one. Call out."

Stilted shacks soon appeared. Swamp-folk clamped their windows shut and slammed their doors as the air-rider flew by. Sea-green gharial and lava-orange, whiskered water cobras slipped through the soggy brush and cut across the water, heavily laden with dead bark.

"There was a giant drake-toad virus outbreak a few years ago," Horace mentioned. "Thousands were hospitalized. Mom worked in the regenerative clinic days straight before Galen developed the cure. But he did, and he saved every infected life except one."

Honor pointed ahead. "I think that's it."

A windmill, its axels swinging wildly in the breeze, loomed at the edge of a mire.

Honor set the air-rider on the bog. The trio unfastened and scrambled to their feet. Honor detached the windgun as Jett and Horace drew toxispray. Back-to-back-to-back, they surveyed the surroundings. Serpents slithered through the water. Patches of grass rustled in the distance.

"Any kappas?" Honor asked.

"None here," Jett said.

"Same," said Horace.

"Let's go."

The trio raced toward a mangrove root cluster with a concealed iron door and mailbox: "G. GALLIPOT, CHEMIZARD."

"Where's the stinking doorbell?" Honor gazed frantically around the mangrove roots.

"I don't see a knocker either," said Horace.

Jett spotted a camouflaged handle in the mangrove. He reached out, uneasy, and tugged it. A low chime rang inside the grotto, followed soon by a bustle. A panel swung open in the iron door. "Whatisit!" A bumpy, gray face with beady emerald eyes glared outward.

Honor cleared her throat. "Mr. Gallipot, you may remember, you may not, but you spoke in my course at Sooth Institute with Professor Magohoot. If you have a moment, I'd like to run something by you."

"Go ahead then," Galen snapped.

"We have an ifrit horn. We'd thought it may be of use."

"Ohhhh. And how did you acquire it?"

"Stumbled across it in Redroot Forest," said Horace.

Galen's eyes ran over the trio. "Sounds stolen."

"It's rightfully ours," Honor promised. "You've our word."

"And whose word might that be?"

"Honor Hane's. My brother, Horace's. And our cousin, Jett's. Doris Gibbons recommended we visit after inspecting the ifrit horn herself."

"Doris read its history? I'll need her letter of authenticity to assure I'm not acquiring contraband." Galen eased. "You can stow that toxispray and windgun. You'll be quite safe inside." The door swung open, revealing the hunchbacked Galen. He had warty skin, scabbed hands, and frayed clothes. He bowed, then receded inward.

Horace's face scrunched. "Ermmm. I don't know about this..."

"Same," muttered Jett.

"Don't be *rude*, boys." Honor prodded their backs, sending them tripping over the doorframe. The grotto was indeed marvelous and scenic. It had warm and cool breezes, cold and hot springs, and sharp stalagmites. Arched walkways interspersed over running waterways. The trio tailed Galen to the largest nook, stuffed with shelves and tables littered with glass bottles, stone cauldrons, old parchment, and begrimed stills. "And if you have any," Honor told him. "I'd like to buy cyanobacteria."

"I've buckets worth, sure. Now, Helga, show me the ifrit horn."

Horace snickered. But Honor and Jett were distracted by the bubbling goblet on the table near Galen. Jett glanced into it and flinched. "Eww. What is that?" The mush looked and smelt like rotten clam chowder.

Galen took a long, clumpy slurp and wiped his mouth. "Troll fat. Highly nutritious. And not bad if you add nectar from a honeypot ant."

Horace ambled to a cauldron full of swirling, mocha plasma.

Galen noticed. "Wait. Don't smell that!" He dashed over. "You could lose your mind! Literally. Azoth and toadstones. Virulent fumes."

Horace swayed back. "Whaaaaoooahhh. I don't feel so good." His face had gone green.

Galen planted Horace on a stool. "Sit, sit. You'll be fine in a minute." He pointed at the trio. "Stop fiddling around in here. This isn't a playset." Galen eased to the cauldron with his nose pinched. "Hmmm... draught water and hair of a manticore ought to do the trick."

"What're you brewing?" Jett inquired.

Galen added draught water. Mocha steam billowed from the cauldron as he plucked precisely six manticore hairs from a glass and dropped them in. The cauldron hissed, frothed, and changed into a poisonous purple color before settling.

"And that is... ?" Jett tried again.

"A special ichor I'm inventing. I hope it will be the remedy for hyoivy. Nasty weed. Fatal in most cases. Now..."

Jett unslung the ifrit horn and set it on the table. Galen unwrapped the scarf and scrutinized the black, engraved horn with bronzed ends.

"It was forged during the Great War," Jett said. "Then—"

"—it was lost," Honor broke in. "Until a pangolin dug it up."

"Mmm hmm, right." Galen was examining the ifrit horn so close the moles on his bumpy nose almost touched it. "Ifrit horns do have their use, though their value diminished when the market for undead antibodies caved—" he drummed his fingers against his grotty lips "—I'd give you... say, fifty elecoin."

"Fifty!" Horace howled, still green. "A teleportation voucher costs five! That ifrit horn has got to be worth five thousand."

"Not to me."

"Give it back then." Horace leapt off the stool, but stopped, the queasiness hitting him, and back-peddled. "You've got a lot of gall trying to take advantage of us."

Galen shrugged and reached for a container of mossy, blue goop. "How much cyanobacteria then, Helga?"

"It's Honor!"

Jett snickered this time. Once Galen sold Honor the cyanobacteria, he forced the trio to the exit. "Next time send a letter instead of wasting my time." He slammed the door closed.

"Odd one, inn't he?" Horace laughed. "Could socialize more."

The heliokinetic suns were now very low. The wind ran so fast it whined.

As the trio headed for the air-rider, a funny feeling overcame Jett. He gazed around the bog, then up at the windmill, and stopped. "It's not moving?" The axels were frozen solid. Honor and Horace paused too and glanced over.

Horace's eyes widened. "Honor, the windgun!"

But Honor was motionless. A spindly, tea-green creature with a barbed tail and diaphanous wings was perched atop the highest axel, staring at them with murderous eyes. The creature leapt into the sky and dove with a terrible screech.

Jett elbowed Honor. "Windgun! Shoot!"

She snapped to as the creature swooped faster and wailed. A deep chugging sound came from the windgun barrel as Honor fired. A vortex of wind unleashed. The creature somersaulted back, mid-air, until the wind stopped. The creature shook its head, screeched, and dove again.

"Turn the dial up all the way," yelled Horace. "No need to play games!"

"*It's on full blast*," Honor screamed back.

Jett numbed. Horace was horror-struck.

"Toxis-s-spray," Honor stuttered.

Jett drew his canister. Horace was quicker. He shot a toxispray stream into the creature's face. It screeched, clawed at its fanged face, and jerked around mid-flight.

"Got 'em!" cheered Horace.

The creature stopped jerking.

"I don't think so." Jett's stomach turned.

The creature barreled into Honor's chest and knocked her to the ground. Its talons ripped into her torso. She cried out horribly.

And in the bottommost pit of Jett's stomach, an untold rage built. A bluish-white energy encapsulated him as a ball of light grew in his hands. With a Herculean yell, Jett released the energy into the creature, vaporizing it in one foul swoop. Jett's breath faded as a cold rush swept through his body and he collapsed on the mire.

6. THE GOOSEFEATHER PUB

"Is he alive?" Horace asked.

"He has a pulse," said Honor. "But he's clammy."

Jett felt a poke on his chest. He groaned, realizing how aware of his bodily functions he was: fast heartbeat, sweaty palms, muscles convulsing.

"Get up," Horace gasped. "We've got to go."

Jett opened his eyes. Horace was kneeling over him, face tense like a hawk. Honor was standing behind Horace, cradling the gashes running from her torso to her arms. She was badly hurt. "Honor you're—"

"—I'll be okay." She surveyed the mire. "The Alluvial Lands aren't safe at night. We've—"

"*Safe*?" said Jett, exasperated. "That kappa could've killed you!"

"That wasn't a kappa," Horace replied, a shadow in his eyes. "That was a gargaunt." He motioned to the windmill, which was spinning again. "A gargaunt in the Alluvial Lands is a bad sign. They live in the Holtmoor, this untamed enclave in the north with acidic bayous."

"Why was it here then? And why'd it attack us?"

"I don't know." Horace helped Jett to his feet. "Support Honor, will you? I need to reinstall the windgun."

Horace hurried to the air-rider as Jett escorted Honor over and harnessed her. Jett and Horace strapped in, and the air-rider lifted into the clouds. The trio sailed in silence for some time; Jett frequently looking over, trying to sense what was running through his new friends' minds. Horace looked unnerved, lost in a train of thought. Honor daubed her cuts and winced, keeping pressure on her worst laceration as she grew paler from blood loss. What was the slumbering power that had awoken in him? The air-rider soared through the outskirts of Recher Town and dipped toward the cottages.

"Uhh-ohh, Horace," Honor murmured.

Mrs. Hane stood rooted in the Hanes's front lawn, a hand against her hip, foot tapping.

"How much trouble are we in?" Jett asked.

"Oh a bit." Horace reduced the speed of their descent. "Anyone have an idea?"

"Like an alibi of where we were?" Jett confirmed. "Could Cape Nautic work?"

Honor groaned beside him. She was desperately white.

"Too far," said Horace. "Besides, visiting the Poltergeist Bomb isn't much better. Plus Honor's cuts aren't explained."

"*Horace*," Mrs. Hane roared from below. "Quit stalling. You land that air-rider this instant."

"We've got to tell Pop about the gargaunt." Honor winced. "And I need mending. Just go."

Horace landed the air-rider on the opposite side of the lawn. Mrs. Hane stormed over. "How dare you—Honor! You're torn to bits!" She wrangled Honor from the harness and rushed her inside without another word.

"We're in it deep." Horace unfastened himself, looking glum.

The boys ventured in.

"Watch your sister," Mrs. Hane demanded. "Make sure she doesn't pass out." Mrs. Hane raced into another room, leaving Honor slumped against a chair in Mr. Hane's study.

"Always overreacting, that one," Honor said with a feeble grin, clothes quite bloody.

"Shouldn't you go to her regenerative clinic?" asked Jett, a wave of guilt flooding him.

Mrs. Hane sprinted back carrying a pinkish-brown serum. She unscrewed the cap and poured it over Honor's most dire laceration. Instantly, it started mending. Jett was stunned.

"*Buffoons*," Mrs. Hane rebuked. "Not you, Jett. Honor. Horace. How could you be so reckless? Tell me what you were doing."

"I was upset about not getting to go to Galen's," Horace said. "Honor caught me trying to sneak Pop's air-rider so she agreed to oversee us."

"A gross miscalculation!"

"It wasn't his fault," Honor managed. "A gargaunt ambushed us."

Mrs. Hane lurched back. "In the Alluvial Lands? Don't be ridiculous."

The trio nodded.

"How can that be?"

"D'you think I'd let a kappa do this to me?" Honor growled.

Mrs. Hane turned to Jett. "What did the creature look like?"

Jett detailed the spindly wings, bowed talons, spired fangs, and munched face.

"And Jett did something amazing, Mom," Horace exclaimed. "Jett saved Honor by releasing a fusion beam!"

Mrs. Hane chuckled. "Horace, be sensible. It's enough trying to convince me of the—"

"—*really*," Honor urged. "It was incredible."

Mrs. Hane stared at Jett with stark admiration. "If that's true, you're incredibly gifted, dear. Thank you for saving my daughter." She beheld the group. "Pop's at Goosefeather. Jett, Horace, stow your things and we'll get a move on." Mrs. Hane removed a piece of minty chocolate from her pocket.

"I don't want any—" Honor shook her head "—I'm better, I swear."

"Who said it's for you?" Mrs. Hane popped the chocolate in her mouth. "Don't think you're getting off this easy, either."

Horace mouthed to Jett, "Told you."

The boys hauled the air-rider into the garage. Jett put the ifrit horn in the Silver Pigeon's basket and Horace placed the cyanobacteria in a temperature-controlled chest, then the group set off for Goosefeather Pub, with Honor walking on her own accord.

By the time they reached a blackened, teak door beneath a hanging sign with a white and gray feather, her lesions had almost disappeared. Laughter streamed onto the street as Mrs. Hane opened the door. Goosefeather Pub was packed with patrons scattered about knotted, teak seats and a long bar. Overhead onyx light fixtures illuminated the room.

"Pop's in back." Horace's voice popped in Jett's mind as they navigated the crowd. "I filled him in on the way over. He checked to see if we would be on time."

"Oho, Jett!" A beanpole man waved at him from a circular booth. He had tufts of marigold hair like Horace and wore a deerstalker cap. The group sat. "Glad you arrived safely from Cape Nautic." He winked. "Like dodo wings? I also ordered woolly mammoth burgers and delectable coconut micro-kraken."

Jett suddenly realized how hungry he was. He hadn't eaten since the caramel on his bed.

The thought of his bed and home saddened him, though he hid it and grabbed a woolly mammoth burger off the platter.

"What a day." Mr. Hane exhaled.

"Indeed," said Mrs. Hane.

"What's that, Hessa?"

"Well... apart from Cape Nautic, your children flew your air-rider to the Alluvial Lands without permission..."

"Where you fought off the gargaunt?" Mr. Hane glanced at Jett with excitement.

"The outcome of the battle is beside the point." Hessa glared. "Reprehensible maneuver, isn't that right?"

Mr. Hane straightened in the booth. "Horace, Honor, mind your mother. And, erm,... follow the rules." He eyed Jett. "Now, how about the story first-hand?"

Jett set down the woolly mammoth burger and swallowed as the Hanes's eyes fell on him. "Well, Mr. Hane, after we left Galen's—"

"No, start from the beginning," said Horace. "How you arrived at Horn House."

"Oh—right."

And so Jett enumerated his tale, Mr. Hane oohhing and aahhing at each twist and turn.

"And I thought I had a wild day," Mr. Hane chuckled after. "Amazing, really. I mean... nearly inconceivable." He paused, as if struck by a mighty thought, then scanned the group with newfound energy. "Jett's story is also a veritable mine of information."

Horace, Honor and Hessa looked lost. Jett was thankful.

"Jett arriving means the Gulog really *did* cross the quantum barrier to Earth that night with Uma Umbra. It means Gene Thorne *wasn't* lying. It means it was the Gulog all along who murdered Ruth Schrödinger."

"Thorne?" Jett repeated. "We met him."

"Sssvr-strrrrk nnn paaapl taaapk." Horace was wolfing down coconut micro-kraken.

"How about not speaking with a full mouth?" Honor snapped.

Horace stuck his tongue out.

"Gross!"

Horace gulped. "The man with silver-streaked hair and the eggplant topcoat? That was Norman, Gene's son."

"Gene was convicted of Ruth's murder because no one could prove the Gulog was present that night," Hessa elaborated. "It was a horrendous time in our history. The incident captured all Pararealm's attention."

"And Uma Umbra?" said Jett.

"She fled," Honor said. "A search party went after her, many died trying to reach Umbra Castle. Uma has never been seen since."

"D'you think Uma's trying to reopen the barrier to Earth?"

"She'd need a Quantum Manipulator, ultra rare ability, unless there's an invocation I'm unaware of. But even then, I can't imagine why. I suppose her motives were unproven the first time though. It was truly a tangled web." Harlow ruminated further. "Regarding the ifrit horn... best you keep it tucked away. No need to talk about it with anyone else for now."

"But Honor wants Norman to appraise it," Horace derided. "She thinks Norman'll pay loads."

"When it sells for eight thousand elecoin you won't be derisive," Honor said back.

"Deceit runs in Norman's blood," Mr. Hane said. "Be wary." His eyes fell on Jett. "You see, it was Norman's grandfather who built our Teleportation Network. It made the Thorne's excessively rich. A wonderful achievement, don't get me wrong, but Norman's grandfather committed patent infringement multiple times to get there. Then Gene, Norman's father, was a furtive ally of Uma Umbra. With Norman... I say it's only a matter of time before something goes awry."

"But Norman reinvigorated Thorne Corp.," Honor professed. "He's done nothing wrong to date. I even hope to work for him one day."

"Word in the Intelligence Service is that Norman cavorts with questionable folk—" Harlow waved a dodo wing "—and he's been seen in shoddy places. Matter of time, I say."

"Innocent until proven guilty," Honor countered.

"Enough," said Hessa. "Harlow, did you sell the tickets?"

Mr. Hane adjusted his napkin-bib. "Got a fair price too."

"Wait. Which tickets?" said Horace.

"With Jett's arrival," said Harlow. "Your mother and I don't think it's prudent to attend the match tomorrow night."

"No!" Horace paused and glanced awkwardly at Jett. "Right, sorry. The Fuzz will check audits when entering the stadium."

"Please go," Jett urged, hit with even more guilt. "You've all done plenty. I can remain at the cottage or something."

Honor slurped lychee juice, looking happy. "Horace has been waiting weeks for The Totem Crusades. Be glad you aren't going."

"You just don't like sports," Horace roared. "You don't appreciate competition."

Honor stared at Jett and ignored her brother. "I compete. And not only that, I win. I'm in the top one percent of my class."

"Boring," Horace barked. "Don't listen to her, Jett. The Totem Crusades are amazing! They're played in this enormous arena, Waropex Garden, whose layout changes each match. There's fire, ice, rock, nighttime, and haze, all with accompanying deities and beasts."

"I suppose we could watch outside the stadium?" Harlow said.

"Alright!" Horace cheered.

"Chill. Mom hasn't said yes," Honor said.

"I guess if you're with them, Harlow, that'd be alright. The park is safe."

"Well then—" Harlow clapped "—with that settled, Jett, tell us about Earth and your family and home. Quietly... of course."

"Well my parents—"

"Their names?"

"Alton and Sheryl."

"Lovely," said Harlow.

It was relaxing, the rest of dinner, as Jett overviewed life on Earth. The Hanes listened intently and asked amusing questions, crinkling their foreheads at everyday things like buses and baseball. With the bill paid, Harlow loosened his belt. "Well, best we're off."

Horace belched.

"*Horace*," Hessa said.

The two suns had gone down. Outside Hane cottage, Harlow held the door for Hessa, Horace, and Honor then pulled Jett into his study. "I can only imagine how you must be feeling," he said. "Had to be a hard shock, winding up in Pararealm. But I'd like to lay out some things."

Jett nodded, unsure what this meant.

"I give you my word: I'll do everything in my power to get you back to Earth. But an Earthling visiting Pararealm is no simple matter, even in times of peace. Boundary Walking is a fickle phenomenon when interworld."

"I understand," Jett said, not reassured.

"Throughout this, I want you to remember that *somehow* you made it here. Which means *somehow* you can make it back." Harlow lent a kind grin. "So, tomorrow for starters, I'll dig through I.S. archives to see if I can pinpoint the origin of Horn House. Perhaps that will guide our search."

"Can I ask you something, Mr. Hane?"

"Please."

"The fusion beam. How did I do that?"

"A redoubtable parapsychic attack." Harlow scratched his cheek. "It's not clear how you summoned that ability. Though perhaps the better question is 'why'?"

"I'm wondering 'why' on a lot of things, like why the Gulog came after me on Halloween."

"There now," Harlow said with empathy. "The Gulog likely sought you out because of your ability. I'm guessing it sort of... sniffed the paranormal prowess in you."

Jett repressed a shudder, thinking about how the Gulog had hunted him.

"And the magic of this 'Halloween' holiday probably heightened the Gulog's sense. Anyway, Hessa has prepared our spare bedroom. Go rest. We can figure out more of this conundrum tomorrow." He escorted Jett down the hall, then rubbed Jett's hair outside the door. "Have a peaceful night. Oh, and, by the way, Newlin has been fed."

"Who?"

"Sleep tight." Harlow strode back toward the study.

Jett unfastened the door. The spare bedroom had a bed like a bird's nest, rustic armoires, a fireplace alight with crackling logs, and a grimy water tank with a great-crested newt swimming tranquilly, who had to be Newlin. Jett dressed in Horace's old pajamas and climbed under the covers. Outside, two half-moons—one steel blue; the other, shimmering tangerine—had settled in the velvety sky laced with twinkling stars, shooting asteroids, and flying chrome saucers zipping about. Despite the coziness and warmth of Hane cottage, Jett had trouble dozing off. His mind kept wandering back to New Orleans. Had his parents noticed he was gone? How much time had passed on Earth? And where, oh where, was the Gulog at this moment?

7. ENOPOLIS

Jett woke to the scarlet and pale suns, feeling as if he'd undergone deep hibernation. He lay in bed for some time ruminating over the events which had unfolded since his arrival, then dressed in a coarse wool sweater and corduroy pants and proceeded into the main area of the cottage.

"Morning. You must be hungry?" Before Jett could answer, Horace had poured him a bowl of Cinnastones—mini, glazed donut and frosted cinnamon cereal. "Quite the ruckus earlier," Horace said, alone. "Surprised you didn't wake. Honor was stressing over her precognition exam, pacing, memorizing study cards. Mom hurried off to a morning shift after oversleeping. Pop was long gone by the time I was awake. But that's a side-show." Horace slurped Cinnastones. "Fire match tonight between the Blackwings and Gremgoblins. Last time my Gremgoblins took a beating, I nearly—"

"—Horace," Jett interrupted. "I'm sure tonight will be great. But, no offense, I'd like to figure out how to get home."

Horace desisted. "Guess I'm being selfish. It's just... it seems like I know you so well already." He nodded, determined. "Don't worry. Pop is on it."

Jett lifted his spoon. "We talked last night."

"Well. *While* Pop figures this out, might as well enjoy yourself. Don't you think?"

Jett took a scoop. The glazed doughnuts and frosted cinnamon were chewy and popped with sweetness. It made him feel better. "Yeah, suppose so." He managed a grin.

After breakfast the boys took the Silver Pigeon to PsyMart to collect the daily deliveries. "Be right back. Guard her, will you?" Horace disappeared through the sliding entrance doors.

Jett stepped off the Silver Pigeon and shoved his hands in his pockets.

"'Ey, Jett." Xander was walking down the sidewalk from a butcher shop, carrying moa filets. His mother was beside him. She had pellucid skin and long incisors as well. "Horace snagging the mail then?"

"Hey, Xander. Yeah." Jett tried to act casual.

"This is Horace's cousin from Cape Nautic," Xander explained to his mom.

Mrs. Dhampir's eyes lingered on Jett. "I wasn't aware the Hanes have family there?"

"My parents sent me here once the Poltergeist Bomb detonated."

An eyebrow rose. "That so?"

"Horace drove by our backyard with Jett, yesterday," Xander said. "In a sour mood as usual."

"Horace on the backroads?" said Mrs. Dhampir. "Even *stranger*. That boy zooms down our street at a million miles per hour—" she scowled at the Silver Pigeon "—leaving tire treads, kicking up muck and leaves. I've spoken with Hessa about it many times. Curious how he... all the sudden... decides to listen."

Jett shrugged. "Ask him."

"Oh, I will." Mrs. Dhampir led Xander away.

Horace soon returned and set the mail bag gently over the ifrit horn in the basket. "What is it?" he asked.

"Xander and his mother came by. Mrs. Dhampir seemed unconvinced of everything."

Horace groaned. "She's so persnickety. Dislikes me more now that I'm suspended." The boys boarded the Silver Pigeon and took off.

***

Jett snatched Odin Stine's mail from the delivery tub and trailed Horace into Redroot Forest.

"Horn House was thattaway?" Horace beckoned north.

"A few hours' walk, yeah," Jett confirmed. "Should we go?"

"It's abandoned." Horace shrugged. "What're we gonna find?" He began climbing a towering sequoia which had a ladder carved into the trunk.

Less confident, Jett followed to the under-balcony of Odin's treehouse.

Horace knocked upward. "Delivery, Odin!"

Footfalls. The under-door opened. "Well, g'morning, Horace."

The boys climbed up. The view was brilliant so high in the treetops.

"Meet Jett," Horace said.

Jett passed Odin his mail. Odin had close-set rheumy eyes, an owlish face, and held a walking cane. "This is Hopie." Odin fished a seed out of his breast pocket and tossed it to the striped-orange warbler on his shoulder. Hopie snatched the seed mid-air and clicked her beak eagerly as Horace strutted toward the window.

"Any luck with the Karmabird today?"

"Only turul this morning. Though that yeti in the Sasqi Mountains has been prowling around an unusual amount."

A long, intricate scope near the window was aimed at the whitecapped Sasqis. A cluttered pile of journals rose next to it from the floor. "That's *some* telescope," said Jett.

"That's an optiscope," Odin corrected. "Captures the entire electromagnetic spectrum." He moseyed over and unhooked the viewing cap. "Have a looksy."

Jett set an eye against the lens and peered at the Sasqis. He saw all sorts of electromagnetic waves and energies, in an array of colors. He stepped back, studied the normal landscape, then again put his eye against the optiscope. "Whoa."

"The Karmabird is translucent unless she chooses not to be," Odin reminded. "The optiscope allows me to see her either way."

"Have you?"

"Once." Odin beamed. "As a boy, leaving Ruth Schrödinger's funeral. The Karmabird drifted across the horizon and left a magnificent golden trail behind her. Despite the circumstances, it was the happiest moment of my life."

"Others saw her as well?" Jett said with surprise.

Odin nodded. "The Karmabird provided many Pararealmians an abundance of hope that day."

"Though there was bandy about it being a shooting star," Horace added. "Or some astrological marvel."

"I know what I saw," Odin averred.

"There've been many 'sightings' through the ages—" Horace primed his fingers, signifying a quote "—but none have been proved."

"Why should they be?" Odin said, looking hurt. "The Karmabird owns no one an explanation. It's to the individual's detriment, not believing."

"Odin," Jett said. "Have you seen anyone... odd roaming around Redroot lately?"

Odin racked his brain. "Not sure what you mean?"

"There's a manor out there—" Jett gestured toward Horn House "—have you seen anyone coming or going?"

"A manor? You're mistaken. My treehouse is the only abode around here. Redroot Forest is a conservatory. Construction is forbidden."

Horace tugged Jett's sleeve and made for the under-door. "Anyway, busy route. See you, Odin."

"Have a spectacular day, boys," Odin said. "And remember: keep your hearts open should you seek the blessings of the Karmabird."

The boys returned to the forest floor. "Why give Odin a hard time?" Jett observed.

"He's myopic with that optiscope. I mean, I believe in the Karmabird, but you don't see me spending my life searching for her." Horace paused at the Silver Pigeon. "Hey! Wanna drive?"

"Really?"

"With the battery charged, just click this button on the handle and we'll zoom away. It's easy."

"But it goes so fast?"

Horace grinned. "Ah, Pop coated the handle with accelesense. Our secret. The gel slows time while you steer. To the driver, we're at normal speed. To everyone else, you're a bullet. And if you want to stop, just let go."

Enthused, Jett saddled on. Horace took the rear. Jett pressed start and the Silver Pigeon rocketed away, blurring the surrounding landscape. Yet the road in front of Jett was crystal clear and navigable. He cruised the thoroughfare with ease. When Mr. Thorne's chateau came into sight, he released the handle, and the Silver Pigeon halted.

"Thatta kid!" Horace leapt off (apparently feeling no nausea), snagged Mr. Thorne's mail, and ascended to the door. The bell rang twice before Horace dropped the mail on the mat and returned. "With nine homes, never know which one Norman's at."

***

Dusk arrived, after Jett spent the afternoon listening to Horace rave about the Totem Crusades while they meandered around Recher Town. He had to admit, with all Horace's babble, he was excited about visiting the arena, Waropex Garden. Horace threw on an emerald-and-violet Gremgoblin jersey (which resembled a rugby shirt), gave Jett a Gremgoblin bobble hat, then dragged Jett out the door with a pair of teleportation vouchers.

PsyMart was bustling, the teleportation line snaked around the corner with Gremgoblin fans.

Jasper—awake and unhappy—was snatching vouchers and teleporting groups to Enopolis at a rapid pace. "Oh, hey, Lowell!" Horace tapped the arm of a tall, good-looking boy in line wearing a Gremgoblin polo. "Odds of victory tonight?"

The boy turned and gave a saintly grin. "Horace! One hundred percent. Blackwings are no match now that the league ditched the salary cap."

Horace was taken aback. "What?"

Lowell laughed. "Where have you been? It's been littered in the games section in *The Focal City Fanzine*... only every day this week." He rubbed Horace's hair like an older brother. "Guess you deliver the mail but don't glean anything from it."

Horace smacked his own forehead. "No wonder Governor Ness picked us. It made no sense when Pop told me."

Lowell leaned closer, whispered, "And you know Governor Ness has insider tips. Rumor is we signed two top players outside the press." He straightened up. "Sorry about Honor by the way. She got overly flustered even though I swore Cora and I were just studying abacomancy. Seriously, that's the truth."

Horace waved affirmation at Lowell as Jasper motioned them into the curved teleportation pod. A vivid, silver flash ported them to Enopolis.

"Anyway," Lowell said. "Meeting my brother in the Thorne Corp. box. Gotsta run." Lowell zipped through the crowd, leaving Jett and Horace in the swarming mass headed toward the lobby. "Grem-goblins, grem-goblins, we are the best," the crowd chanted. "Gremgoblins, gremgoblins, we'll put the Blackwings to rest!"

"Lowell'll play in the Totem Crusades one day," Horace told Jett amidst the electricity. "Already being scouted by the league."

The boys exited PsyMart. Soaring towers lined the impeccable, clean street which fed to a behemothic, watermelon-shaped stadium with thousands of windows, Waropex Garden. Horace pointed to a beatific park nearby. "Pop's at Thule Grounds. Just mindlinked me."

The boys wrestled through the scuttling people and found Harlow, in a Gremgoblin deerstalker cap, waving at lawn's edge. "Stellar spot for us near the screen," Harlow said. "You two holding up alright?" He led the boys into the park.

"Welcome, welcome, welcome," the announcer said on the jumbotron. "To tonight's

Totem Crusade. With a fire arena drawn by the Blackwing captain, you know the match will be grueling, and heated." (Crowd laughter). "On one side, the Nimadora Blackwings; the other, the Santomite Gremgoblins." The camera changed, revealing the titan-sized pitch of lava pits, jutting magnetite rocks, and fiery beasts (like a snapping tortoise swimming in a pool of magma). "And, here, we, go!" the announcer said. The Totem Crusades were underway.

***

Full of vim and vigor, the victorious Gremgoblin fans headed toward the exit of Thule Grounds, dodging unruly Blackwing supporters. With seconds remaining, the Gremgoblins had retrieved the Blackwing statue of a raven to secure the win.

"Oh, man," Horace cheered. "What a grab by McGuiness!"

"What's that up there?" Jett asked.

"What a grab," Horace repeated, arms raised.

"Mr. Hane—"

The intersection outside Thule Grounds was gridlocked. Fans were waffling and emphatically pointing at something on the ground, faces staggered.

"Must be a brawl," said Horace. "Happens often."

The crowd thickened as Jett, Horace, and Harlow moved closer.

"I'm not so sure, boys. Stay close." Harlow drew his Intelligence Service badge and forged his way through. "I.S., I.S., let me by people, let me by." Fans in the inner circle had cameras out and were snapping photos. Others had their eyes up, scanning windows and the rooftop of Enopolis Radio Tower. Suddenly, Harlow whirled around and motioned the boys back. "Horace, get Jett home, now." Jett peered around Harlow. A woman was face-down on the concrete in a pool of blood. Her legs and arms were folded wrong. Camera flashes clicked. "Go," Harlow insisted.

Jett turned with Horace and began twisting through the flocking crowd.

"Side entrance of PsyMart's this way," Horace shouted, moving fast.

"Horace, slow down," Jett cried, jogging to keep up.

A drunken Blackwing fan collided with him and knocked him down. "Ow!" His elbow pulsed with pain. He glanced up from the concrete. "Horace!" His friend's outline faded in the shifting mass. "Horace? Wait! HORACE."

Jett pushed himself to his feet. He spun and debated returning to Harlow, but the crowd was swelling and growing more tumultuous, so Jett pressed on, assuming Horace would be waiting. "Horace?" Jett called at the crowd edge, appraising the scene. "Horace?" But there were no rosy cheeks. No mop of tousled, marigold hair nearby. Jett hurried to a far-off lamppost and turned toward the scene, panicking, yearning for his friend to emerge from the madness. A door burst open behind him. Jett pivoted toward it.

In the alley beside Enopolis Radio Tower, a freight door swung shut and someone in a hooded, rust-orange tunic was sprinting the other way. Startled, Jett glanced back and saw that no one else had noticed. He trotted toward the alley as the tunicked person careened around the corner. Jett followed. He planted himself at the bend and poked his nose out. The tunic was stopped at a light at the next intersection, staring across the street at Fuzz officers galumphing along, holding their police belts, panting. Pedestrians strolled down the sidewalk, ignorant to the mania a street over. Jett walked out of the alley and approached the tunic with caution.

"Ex-excuse me?" he stammered. "I'm l-lost. Could you tell me where's PsyMart?"

The tunic turned. Jett was surprised that in the hood was a winsome woman with tangles of teal hair and silvery eyes. An iridium choker wrapped her neck. She was alert. Jett watched her consider whether to answer. "I'm not from here," she stated. "I wouldn't know."

"Please... I need to teleport home. I got separated from my family."

"You shouldn't talk to strangers." She glanced behind Jett into the alley.

"But I need help."

"You're alone?"

"Yes."

"Jett?"

Norman Thorne strutted out of a fancy timepiece store. His ambiance was impressive. Relief washed over Jett. "Mr. Thorne, I got split up. This woman was helping me."

Mr. Thorne glanced at her, skeptical, and extended his hand. "Norman Thorne. Don't believe we've met."

"Toko." Their hands released. "This boy asked for aid."

"I need to find Horace," Jett urged. "He's bound to stay in Enopolis searching for me."

Mr. Thorne locked eyes with Toko. "I'll help the boy. You're relieved of your duty."

Toko nodded and hurried away.

"Mr. Thorne," Jett said, anxious. "A woman fell off Enopolis Radio Tower. Toko slipped out of a backdoor in the alley beside it."

"You followed her alone?"

"Well, yes."

"Stupid. Especially with your situation. I commend your bravery though. Thank you for bringing it to my attention." He took Jett by the shoulder. "Let's get you to Recher Town. Horace will work things out." He marched toward PsyMart. "The woman who died. Did anyone recognize her?"

"Not that I heard."

"Did you see her face?"

"It was turned the other way. And distorted."

At the teleportation pod on the fifth floor of PsyMart, Mr. Thorne presented the attendant a unique black voucher which granted them private access.

"How come you weren't at the match?" Jett asked as the curved door closed.

"Who says I wasn't earlier?"

"Oh."

"Not that it's your business, Jett, but I was met my advisor at The Elebank at halftime." A silver flash of light blinked them to Recher

Town. Jett and Mr. Thorne departed and passed a sleeping Jasper.

"I was wondering," Jett said. "Do you have any idea how I can get home?"

"I've been considering your situation to a great degree," Mr. Thorne said. "More than one recent event has rung a distant bell in my personal history. I will back to you, as I said. There are particulars I still need to parse through." Outside Hane Cottage, Mr. Thorne bowed. "I'll speak with the authorities about Toko. You should call it a night."

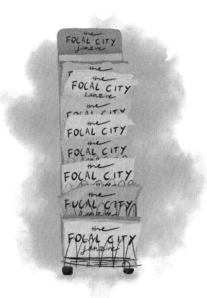

8. BAD PUBLICITY

Jett woke the next morning feeling ill-equipped. Hessa had been irate when Harlow and Horace returned without Jett and had impressed upon Harlow how rash it had been sending the boys off before she lamented further disappointment in Horace. Once tempers abated, Jett had recounted how he tailed Toko and ran into Mr. Thorne, then Harlow detailed what had transpired at the crime scene, sharing that the dead woman was one Rinona Hollygrew, a wanted taintist (someone who willingly spreads disease and poison). Witnesses had sworn that Rinona flew from the roof of Enopolis Radio Tower but hadn't seen how and certainly didn't know why. No more clarity had been gained at the time.

Jett continued digesting all this as he entered the sitting room. Hessa, Honor, and Horace were mid-deliberation.

"No roaming anymore—" Hessa pointed a stiff finger at Horace "—with the kerfuffle last night... finish your route and stay home. Honor will stop by during a class break."

"I will?" Honor asked.

"And one more thing—" Mrs. Hane moved to the entryway closet "—don't forget: this evening is our family portrait." She ferreted through and removed pineapple-yellow overalls and a checkered bow tie. "Horace, I want you dressed and your hair combed when I get home. No 'ifs', 'ands', or 'buts'."

Horace's eyes became enormous. "Mom, *no.*"

Honor exploded with laughter. "That's the lamest outfit I've ever seen!"

"I'll wear what I have on," Horace pleaded.

"No you will not." Hessa withdrew a dainty, marmalade-orange sundress with ivory fringe-work. "And Honor, and this is—"

"—not what I'm wearing. It's *horrid.*"

Horace grabbed his belly, cackling. "That's worse than mine!"

"Err, Mrs. Hane," Jett said. "Did Mr. Hane go to Cape Nautic this morning? I was hoping to talk to him."

"Harlow was put in charge of the Rinona Hollygrew investigation," she said with pride. "Dressed and hair done when I get home," she repeated to her kids and exited. Honor soon left with an armful of textbooks. The boys ate their Cinnastones and boarded the Silver Pigeon for PsyMart to collect deliveries.

Two blocks past Goosefeather Pub, an elephantine man with stubby orange hair ambled out of a newsstand. His nose was glued to *The Focal City Fanzine*.

"Oi! Watch it, Magohoot," Horace shouted and swerved to a stop.

Professor Magohoot glimpsed up. "Ay, sorry, Horace. I'm reading this—" He noticed Jett. His eyes flew to the newspaper cover. "—it's you!"

Jett's face scrunched. "What?"

Professor Magohoot jabbed at the newspaper. Jett hopped off the Silver Pigeon and took the *Fanzine*. On the front page was a photo of him peering around Harlow in the inner ring of the crime scene under Enopolis Radio Tower.

INTELLIGENCE SERVICE'S HANE LEADING HOLLYGREW CASE, read the headline. Jett stared, dumbstruck. His brain was filled with a blank buzzing. "This can't be..."

"Must have been quite the scene," Professor Magohoot said. "Sure makes you wonder if Rinona jumped." He leaned his enormous body over and whispered, "Did you see her fall?"

Jett shook his head.

Professor Magohoot frowned. "I get it. Save the scoop for the press. Fine." He checked his bronze pocket watch. "Good lord, I've got to run." Professor Magohoot hitched up his trousers and tromped away, shaking the street with each massive footfall.

"What do we do?" Jett said. "Horace—" Jett poked him "—what is it?"

"Shhh."

Horace suddenly pulled Jett back on the Silver Pigeon. "Word's out! Time to bolt." He turned the Silver Pigeon around, hit the accelerator, and rocketed toward Redroot Forest.

"Where are we going?" Jett shouted over the wind, fighting his stomach.

Horace sped up.

"What's happening?"

The Silver Pigeon stopped. Jett stumbled onto the lawn outside Mr. Thorne's chateau. Horace leapt off and walked the Silver Pigeon up the driveway. Jett scrambled after him. "Horace, can you please tell me what's happening?"

"The Governor's Office knows you're *untested*," Horace said. "Someone close to Governor Ness saw the *Fanzine* and started asking questions. They're interrogating Pop!"

Jett's heart sunk. "How do you know?"

"Pop's not the *only* telepath at the I.S.," Horace snapped. "The Fuzz are heading to our cottage right now!"

The air swept from Jett's lungs. "I—I'm sorry, Horace, I—"

"It's not your fault. But we had to be off." Horace gestured to Mr. Thorne's chateau. "This was the first place I thought of." Horace parked the Silver Pigeon behind the hedges. Jett grabbed the ifrit horn from the tub and slung it over his shoulder. Horace rapped on the backdoor.

"What are we doing?" Jett asked.

"I don't know exactly." Horace rapped once more.

Mr. Thorne appeared out of a back room. He studied the boys from afar, then stormed over.

"Jett's been made," Horace cried. "He's on the front page of the *Fanzine*!"

Mr. Thorne absorbed this. He surveyed Redroot Forest behind them with suspicion. "Why come here, Horace?"

"The Governor's Office has Pop. The Fuzz are coming to Recher Town now. I didn't know where else to go."

"Honor raves about your resourcefulness," Jett added.

Mr. Thorne waved them in. "Where are Hessa and Honor now?"

"Soothe Institute. Mom's at the clinic."

Mr. Thorne brooded over something. Consternation came and left his face. "Boys, there's something I must show you." His eyes averted behind his circular eyeglasses. He about-faced and led them to an underground hallway. "There are despotic things happening in the depths of Focal City; things far worse than the public believes." The hallway led to a chamber with a private teleportation pod. "When my grandfather built Pararealm's teleportation infrastructure, he created a secret network of unregistered pods in inconspicuous locations. Few know this." Mr. Thorne booted up the control panel and powered the pod on. "I'm sending you somewhere safe. I'll fetch Hessa and Honor and link up with you as a quick as possible." He pushed them inside. The curved door closed. Mr. Thorne tapped several buttons on the panel, and a moment later, Jett and Horace were gone.

9. THE ISLE

The private pod fizzled. Jett and Horace exited into a dark stone chamber, silent save the sound of sloshing waves. Jett went to an open-air window and stared at white-capping ocean spray. The sky was pallid with pending rain. "Horace—!"

Beneath the window was no esplanade, only jutting boulders forming an isle shore. Horace moved beside him. "I think we're in the Diluvian Sea."

"But *where* are we?" Jett asked.

The boys left the stone chamber for a gusty courtyard, which had five floors of interior walkways and several guard-housed turrets. The courtyard was deserted. The boys wandered across it, glancing down halls and scanning the towers, as a cheer arose from the southeastern corner of the fort. They hurried over. Jett peered through a slit in a hoary door.

"What's in there?" whispered Horace, unnerved.

"Can't see. The crack's too thin." Jett stepped back.

Horace inched forward and—*creakkkk*—he leaned against the door slightly.

"HUSH," came a voice. "Someone's listening." The door ripped open. A crowd in rust-orange tunics goggled at the boys, many fingered an array of weapons, others strained their necks to get a look and whispered urgently. "Who are you?" demanded the man.

"Norman Thorne sent us," Jett said. "We're sorry to intrude. We weren't aware—"

"Jett?" A woman moved forward. She had teal hair and an iridium choker.

"Toko?"

The leader called to her. Knurled, graying hair fell to his shoulders. "You know them?"

"One, yes," Toko replied.

The chamber breathed relief as Toko swept through the crowd. "What're you doing here?"

"Mr. Thorne will explain." Jett was anxious. "Where, uhhhh, are we?"

"Why, the Isle of Iconoclasts!" The leader at the head table bowed and gave a merry chuckle. "Reese Schrödinger, at your service."

"Reese Schrödinger?" said Horace. "*You're* an Iconoclast?"

Reese grinned. "Naturally."

"I thought the Iconoclasts kidnapped your daughter?"

"Mere propaganda meant to frame us as the enemy, I'm afraid. As is true of the Poltergeist Bomb detonated in Cape Nautic." Reese surveyed the courtyard. "Norman isn't with you?"

"He went for my mom and sister, Hessa and Honor Hane," Horace explained. "I don't understand... how is Mr. Thorne associated with the Iconoclasts? You're the bad guys!"

Laughter filled the chamber.

"Who do you think funds our effort?" Toko said. "The Isle was once a disused fort from the Great War. The Thorne's acquired it, hypothesizing a logistical use for the corporate empire, but nothing came of it. Norman had the Isle designated a historical landmark and forbade visitation."

"But *you're* the bad guys," Horace repeated.

"Who refuse to succumb to draconian law?" asked Reese. "Who reject the corruption so steeped in our government? Who seek to free the hundreds quietly imprisoned by Governor Ness and his Fuzz officers for some ruthless reason?" He wended around the table and moved closer. "There is much you must unlearn, boy. When Riley disappeared, it was *Norman* who aided me. We had always respected each other, but our bond grew from the mutual loss of loved ones."

"I'm not following," Horace ceded.

"Deep in his heart, Norman believes Uma Umbra had his father under a mind control spell. He believes that Uma walked his father to his death that night with Ruth, my late wife. Just like I believe Governor Ness swept Riley's kidnapping under the rug as a directive from his master, the very same Uma Umbra."

"You think she's alive?" Jett surmised.

"Uma's thriving." Reese held up his pointer finger. "The Iconoclasts have forensic evidence through our plants in the I.S. Intercepted transmissions, redacted letters."

"You said not to worry about Uma," Jett gasped at Horace. "You said everyone accepts she's dead and buried."

"Governor Ness is but her puppet," said Toko.

"What about your daughter?" asked Horace.

"I pray for answers every night," Reese said, quite glum.

Jett turned to Toko, realizing. "You were on the roof with Rinona Hollygrew, weren't you? And bumping into Mr. Thorne wasn't coincidence."

"Rinona was hired to kidnap Riley." Toko nodded with despondency. "She leapt off Enopolis Radio Tower before I could question her. She was a heartless coward."

"She feared Uma Umbra," someone growled.

A stone-faced Mr. Thorne and a terrified Honor were in the doorway.

"Indeed," said Reese.

Honor rushed forward and flung her arms around Jett. "I'm glad you made it. It's a circus in Recher Town. The Fuzz are checking every cottage for you and my brother."

"Where's Mom?" Horace asked.

Honor sobbed. "The Fuzz took her to Focal City. Mr. Thorne and I barely escaped."

"We'll free your parents. And all the others wrongfully imprisoned," Reese pronounced to the room. "Norman, the time has come to collect the fifth and final parastone and proceed with our stratagem."

Mr. Thorne revealed from under his eggplant topcoat a magnificent, luminous bow. "The unmissable instrument," he presented. "To be traded to Queen Triton for her waterstone."

"Hold on—" Honor wiped a tear "—Reese, are you trying to resurrect your wife?" She glanced at Jett and Horace. "Mr. Thorne filled me in."

"Clearly more than us," Jett returned.

"The five parastones of Pararealm," Toko elucidated. "Magma, pearl, leaf, moon, and water. Individually, each increases the holder's ability in that medium. Together, the quintet has the power to bring someone back to life."

"We've worked to locate them for years," Mr. Thorne said. "Yesterday, I left the Totem Crusades to pick up the Zephyr Bow, acquired by my Elebank advisor from a Drakenberg merchant for an unconscionable sum."

"But *who* are you resurrecting?" Honor probed.

"Nagato," said Reese. "The Shadow Bender of legend."

"Nagato carried out the stealth mission to Umbra Castle during the Great War," Toko added. "It was Nagato who slayed our enemy."

Honor was stunned. "You expect him to do so again?"

"In Nagato's veins run noble blood. He was a warrior for the people, a defender of liberty."

"But he was betrayed!"

"But not by us," said Reese.

Honor's brow furrowed, as if recalling something deep in her mind. "Why go through so much effort to collect the parastones? There are faster and simpler ways to resurrect the dead."

"We have no interest in necromancy," Reese asserted. "It's a wicked practice."

"Necromancy revives only the soul," said Toko. "It is a cruel art."

"Speaking of necromancy," Mr. Thorne said. "Jett, I assume you haven't told the group what lies on your shoulder? Nor have you recounted who you are?"

Jett unslung the ifrit horn and unwrapped the scarf. "I discovered this in an abandoned house in Redroot Forest. Horn House, as we call it, appears on no map. According to a psychometrist, this ifrit horn once belonged to Uma Umbra."

Reese studied the artifact with trepidation. "How is it you came to be there?"

"I traveled to Redroot Forest... from Earth."

Gasps. Reese looked like he misheard. "*Earth*?"

The Iconoclasts huddled around Jett as he apprised them of his encounter with the Gulog on Halloween, crossing into Pararealm through the portal under his bed, and all the subsequent events which led to him standing in the Isle. The retelling caused a remarkable sensation, leaving the entire chamber openmouthed.

"This is *most* irregular," Reese said after. "Given what we've heard," he told the Iconoclast faction, "it is clear Uma Umbra is again attempting to open the quantum barrier to Earth. Well, more than attempting," he corrected. "Uma was successful. What I don't understand is how." He beheld the chamber. "I hope Uma has not leveraged some unknown, dark practice which would allow her to Quantum Manipulate. The thought scares me." Reese smiled at Jett. "Thankfully, this young Kinetic Channeler arrived instead of the murderous Gulog. Perhaps the Karmabird has summoned Jett to Pararealm for aid."

Kinetic Channeler? Jett thought.

"Time is scarcer than we realized!" Reese raised a fist in the air. "Norman, retrieve the waterstone from Queen Triton. We will continue operations at the Isle in the meantime."

The Iconoclasts clapped and hoorayed.

Mr. Thorne motioned to a petite woman with violet eyes, a violet ponytail, and a pale complexion. She followed Mr. Thorne, Toko, Jett, Honor, and Horace into the courtyard and shut the chamber door.

"Panoplía, could you outfit these three?" Mr. Thorne looked to Toko. "We'll need a parascouter. Grab windguns from the Foundry. Meet you in the hangar." He hustled away.

Panoplía approached Horace. "Hold steady." She outlined Horace's body, and, amazingly, a rust-orange tunic amalgamated over his frame. "Your bastioarmor tunic will shield against minor paranormal attacks, but it's not invincible. Now, how does it fit?"

Horace fidgeted, inspecting it. "Err. It's not really my color..."

Panoplía repeated the process for Jett and Honor. "Please excuse me. I must return to the Assembly Room." She ventured back into the turret base.

Toko escorted the trio to the Foundry, a shadowy basement replete with firepits, casting tools, and odd CPUs. She waved at a stout woman molding a mace and plucked an ash-colored cylindrical gun from a rack.

"That's a windgun?" Jett asked.

"A Thorne Corp. industrial prototype." Toko pointed at a dial beside the safety. "At max power, this will send someone halfway across Pararealm. Do *not* take them off safety unless Norman and I are disabled or give you approval. Do *not* expect to use it." She stared at the trio. "Repeat that."

"We are not to take the windgun off safety without approval," they obliged together. "We do not expect to use them."

Toko smiled and allotted each a weapon. "Good. Let's get moving."

Jett followed Toko, Horace, and Honor down a stairwell to the hangar. "How come we aren't teleporting out?" he asked Mr. Thorne.

"The Mystlands aren't industrialized. Hence the parascouter." Mr. Thorne brandished a white spherical device with a green screen, like a high-tech compass. He hit 'OPEN' on the wall. The massive door rose, sending sunlight cascading over a sky-blue tiltrotor helicopter on the helipad. "The Condor," Mr. Thorne presented. "Equipped with active camouflage. She resembles a fast-moving cloud in the sky." Mr. Thorne took the pilot seat, Toko, the co-pilot. Jett, Horace, and Honor hopped in the rear. "Buckle up," Mr. Thorne said, flicking on the tiltrotor and active camouflage. The Condor lifted and glided out of the hangar into the clouds with ease.

"Pop and I do fishing trips off Cape Nautic." Horace nodded toward the mainland shore, far away. "Plenty of sawtooth sharks in the Diluvian Sea, along with cetus whales and narwhals. I hope he's alright."

The cerulean-blue sea soon morphed into a dense land of geysers and bright-green tropics. Mr. Thorne snaked into the Mystlands, following an emerald river full of highlighter-yellow eels and pink, horned fish. Enormous, waxy tee frogs leapt between branches and crept along slimy vines. Kite-sized rainbow moths fluttered over the canopy. The farther the Condor flew, the more peaceful the Mystlands grew. At last, Mr. Thone lowered toward a box canyon with a soaring waterfall and sparkling lagoon. The Condor thudded to a halt. "Never have managed the landing," he chuckled and unstrapped.

Jett hopped out and caught a manatee with ivory antenna in the lagoon waving at him. He grinned and waved back as Toko directed them onto a footpath leading into the waterfall. In the wet treescape, lime-green women wearing moss and leaves were staring. "Dryads," Toko mentioned. "Women of the Mystlands. Not combative."

The group spun, hearing a fall.

"Help!" Horace shouted. A vine was wrapped around his ankle and was dragging him into the trees. At the end of the vine loomed a bulbous, six-petalled flower with teeth. "*Help*," Horace screamed again, grappling at the dirt.

From her tunic, Toko drew a gleaming sword and sliced the vine in half. The flower squealed. The vine thrashed and receded into the thicket as a gluey pickle-green secretion sept from Horace's gash. Toko knelt and lifted his leg. She studied the secretion. "I don't know what this is. Norman?"

Horace wailed in pain.

"Not my area of expertise." Mr. Thorne scanned around rapidly.

"I need to extract the barbs," Toko told Horace, who pounded the soil in agony.

"Just do it!"

"One... two—" Toko yanked the spurs out. Horace howled louder.

A dryad glided over and clasped a tree. "Scorpionshood," she said airily.

"*Help me*," Horace cried.

"You must see Queen Triton," the dryad muttered. "Before your throat closes permanently."

Toko heaved Horace up and dashed toward the waterfall. Jett, Honor, and Mr. Thorne followed. The footpath rose beyond the lagoon into an amber-colored cave with steamy chambers and superheated pools. Deep inside, Queen Triton was perched on a throne carved into rock, half-submersed in hot water. She had scarred, azure skin, plum scales, a muscular tale, and she clutched a golden trident with silver tips in one hand. Other triton surrounded their Queen, lapping in the pools and hopping between.

"Scorpionshood!" Toko bellowed, jumping across the rock path. "Queen Triton, help us!"

"The boy's suffering means nothing to me," Queen Triton hissed, her tail slithering. She motioned at the Zephyr Bow held by Mr. Thorne. "That is my sole concern."

"Please." Toko shifted Horace in her arms. "This boy's done nothing to wrong you."

"But what recompense do I get?"

Mr. Thorne fished out his parascouter. "This. It detects all nearby human-like lifeforms and contains a detailed map of Pararealm." He clicked it on and threw it to Queen Triton, who snatched it with ease. "It will strengthen the Mystland's defense."

Queen Triton scrutinized the parascouter then murmured something to nearby kin. A teenage triton swam away and returned a moment later. Horace's wails echoed in the steam, as the triton then swam out to Toko. "Eat the marvelberry." The triton shoved puce-colored fruit into Horace's mouth. "*Chew*." Pale and sweaty, Horace munched and swallowed. "And a delicashroom." The triton jammed a tye-dye mushroom through his lips. Horace gulped, and soon, the color lifted back into his face. Toko set him on his feet but kept supporting him.

"Close one," Horace said, eyes red and smile droopy.

"Thank you, Queen Triton." Mr. Thorne stepped forward and held up the luminous Zephyr Bow. "The unmissable instrument. I hereby endow it to you under the terms of our long-standing arrangement. The Zephyr Bow for your waterstone."

Queen Triton flapped her tail. "I've been thinking... why go to such lengths to acquire the Zephyr Bow for me? We both know it is far more valuable..."

"Value is relative, my Queen," Mr. Thorne countered.

Queen Triton hissed but said nothing else.

"The Umbras are back."

Hisses filled the dank chamber. "The Umbras you claim..."

"I know our species have not seen eye to eye," Mr. Thorne said with an air of dignity. "But you must remember how close we all came to losing when the Umbras had power. A queen with such perspective will appreciate the dangers slumbering in the High East."

"Very well," Queen Triton grunted. "After all, we tritons place great significance on our word. This does not make us allies though."

"But perhaps it might make us lesser foes." Mr. Thorne walked the Zephyr Bow to Queen Triton. She scrutinized the instrument, turned it over thrice, and nodded.

10. THE SHADOW BENDER

The entire Iconoclast faction had gathered in the Isle courtyard as Mr. Thorne laid the marbled, teal waterstone in a chest beside the four other parastones.

"Iconoclasts," Reese announced. "At dawn, we will take part in the rarest of Pararealm ceremonies. Tonight: feast, rest, celebrate... for the tides of our campaign are about to change."

The Iconoclasts applauded and marched toward the mess hall. Huge bowls of megalodon stew lined the communal tables. The trio sat down with Toko.

"Has anyone from the I.S. reached out?" Jett asked Horace.

"Mindlink isn't possible at the Isle," Toko replied. "Teleblockers mounted throughout the fort. Along with a multitude of other defense protocols."

Honor sighed.

"We'll get word soon," Toko assured.

"How did you track Rinona?" asked Jett.

"I'm a bounty hunter," Toko said, sipping stew. "I led the private search for Riley years ago. Didn't take long to determine Rinona was involved. She bragged of her work in disreputable circles. Imprudent habit."

"So what happened?" Honor asked.

"Rinona somehow caught word I was onto her. Trail went cold. Eventually, a rumor surfaced that Rinona was hiding under the name 'Humbert' in the Drakenbergs. I staked out what I thought was the right shanty for weeks but never saw anyone. So I started writing letters acting like Ostrog Shaughnessy—a known accomplice of Uma Umbra—citing details about Riley's kidnapping that only someone intimate would have. Claimed I had a job for her." Toko leaned closer. "After a few back-and-forths, we agreed to meet atop Enopolis Radio Tower while folks were at the Totem Crusades. I wasn't sure Rinona would show, but when she walked through the maintenance door she recognized me." Toko shook her head. "Rinona had zero remorse. Before I could convince her to come with me, she leapt. I gained no further knowledge on Riley."

"She was scared of Uma Umbra?" asked Jett.

"Seems to be the case," replied Toko.

"You all, a minute?" Mr. Thorne was at the mess hall door.

"What for? I'm eating."

"*Horace*," Honor retorted.

Mr. Thorne escorted the foursome to a fire-lit den full of buttoned couches and wingback seats. In one was Reese, holding a stiff drink and staring into the fireplace.

"I've waited half my life for redemption... cooped on this Isle." Flamelight flickered off Reese's face. "Once Nagato slays Uma Umbra, I'm ordering an assault on that puppet Governor of hers. He deserves more than death for his betrayals." Reese tossed a letter on the logs. It bloomed and curled into embers.

"The Hane children and Jett are here," Mr. Thorne reminded.

Reese turned. His eyes were glazed, like he was coming out of a reverie. Jett gave a meek grin which Reese didn't reciprocate. "Fenton Warbler, a trusted telepath in the I.S., sent word," he said to Honor and Horace. "Your parents have been charged with violating the Ordinance of Order via aiding and abetting an 'untested'." Honor grabbed Jett's arm. Horace stared in a daze. "If Governor Ness knew Jett's from Earth, I fear the situation would be far more grave. Regardless, Harlow's arrest has spawned a rift in Focal City. Top brass across the government are quitting." Reese took a long drink. "I sought to give you an update first-hand. We've arranged bunks in the barracks. Get some rest."

Toko led the trio across the courtyard under a star-strewn indigo sky. "Ever since Riley was taken, Reese has spent too much of his time plotting," Toko observed minutes later, at a corner of unoccupied bunks. "Perhaps some of his thinking is correct, but much of it is clouded by grief and anger." Toko bowed and receded, leaving the trio alone in the barracks.

Jett unslung his ifrit horn and windgun, tossed off his tunic, and dropped into a bottom bed. Horace climbed on top. Honor took the lower frame beside them.

"I don't want to stay here," she said. "Being at the Isle makes us accomplices."

"You want to leave?" Horace probed.

"We haven't done anything wrong. You and I could go to the I.S."

Jett's stomach fell with unease.

"You want to *turn yourself in*?" Horace said.

"I want to be rational," Honor went on. "Read between the lines, Horace: we're in the midst of a coup d'état."

Horace leaned over the bunk bars. "D'you honestly think going to the I.S. is an option? D'you think you can just mosey up to Reese or Mr. Thorne and say 'Hey, it's been great getting to know the ins and outs of your secret base, but we'd like to be off now. Mind dropping us ashore?' NO. We're in this thing. The only way out is forward." Horace fell back on his pillow. "Besides, with the Shadow Bender, our job is just to wait."

"We don't know if the Shadow Bender will fight for the Iconoclasts. What if he wakes from the afterlife and attacks *us*?"

"That a possibility?" Jett asked.

"The Shadow Bender was such an insuperable force when he was alive... even after he single handedly disassembled the Umbra's, Prince Icarus executed him for fear that he would one day seize power."

Jett gulped.

"And at dawn," Honor went on. "The Icono-clasts are bringing Pararealm's greatest warrior back from the grave."

Jett gulped again. "Honor, Horace, there's still one thing I don't understand."

"Then you've got this more figured out than me," said Horace.

"All those years ago... and now... why is Uma Umbra tampering with the quantum barrier to Earth?"

***

Enthusiastic murmurs spurred Jett from sleep. The barracks were a blur of rust-orange tunics headed out the door. Jett rolled over, gazed out-side, and listened to the lapping waves. The two moons had almost set and ochre clouds were scudding across the horizon on this nascent day.

"I didn't mean to intimate that we'd abandon you." Jett swung his head in the other direction. Honor was dressed and seated at the edge of her made bed. "It's just—"

"—I know." Jett stretched awake. "It's alright."

Honor gave a small grin of thanks. "Horace, everyone's in the courtyard. We're behind."

Horace groaned.

Honor set her feet on Jett's mattress and pulled herself up. "Get up, Horace."

"Ugggh, it's so early," Horace fussed. "Why does this stupid ceremony have to be at dawn?"

"Do you want to miss it?"

Jett threw on his tunic.

Horace yawned and rolled over. "Uhm, I don't mind."

"Get out of bed!"

The Iconoclasts were gathered around the chest of parastones. The courtyard was frigid. Reese paced before the chest, clutching an archaic book. "Eternal magmastone, we summon your vigor in this dark hour," he orated. "Eternal pearlstone, we summon your wisdom in this time of peril—" The ocean churned with sweeping, white moves as Reese proceeded with the venerations for each parastone. He then stepped away. The parastones glowed. The sky tinged overhead. Clouds thickened and swirled. "Oh, great parastones," Reese chanted. "We ask that you resurrect from the dead... Nagato the Shadow Bender, defender of Pararealm and her people!" The ocean surged. Salty mist sprayed over the fort's high walls as waves the size of houses flared with foam. A tree in the courtyard broke. The crack sounded like an explosion. The parastones flashed with electricity. A tornado reigned down from the sky and encircled the chest. The tornado howled with a supernal energy, its wind thick with dirt and leaves. The Iconoclasts were driven back by its ferocity.

Then.

The tornado lifted. The clouds thinned and the burgeoning rays of morning suns warmed the courtyard, revealing the outline of a strapping man. Draped in a black yoroi with a hooded cowl and clenched kusarigama blades (razor-sharp sickles fixed to long chains), the Shadow Bender unfurled his arms in the haze.

"Where am I?" His voice was stentorian. He glared at the Iconoclasts with metallic yellow eyes, face tenser than a bowstring.

Reese inched closer. "Great Shadow Bender, we have summoned you back to life because Pararealm again needs your bravery. The Umbras have returned, Nagato."

Nagato flexed his arms and tightened his grip on his kusarigama blades. "Pararealm was consumed by hate when I was alive. Battles raged. Tens of thousands perished in the Great War before I alone slayed Urien and Ursa Umbra in the High East... only to be betrayed. You have heaved me from eternal peace and expect me not only to fight but to trust you. Why?"

"Pararealm has no kings, no prince to back-stab you, only a fraying democracy," Mr. Throne stated, stepping forward. "Treachery and deceit are growing. Innocent people's lives are being destroyed. We don't ask you to fight for us, Shadow Bender. We ask that you do what is noble... what is right."

Nagato studied Mr. Thorne fiendishly, then scrutinized the broader Iconoclasts. His metallic eyes landed on Jett before falling back onto Reese. "Tell me: what have the Umbras done this time?"

***

In the Assembly Room, Nagato detailed his clandestine journey to Umbra Castle and recounted how he had snuck from a hermitage in Enopolis through the Zodiac Desert into the High East "—that is the only way to arrive unseen," Nagato avouched, running a kusarigama over the map. "Caroten Lake lies in front of the crags which lead to Umbra Castle, rendering it impossible to not be exposed from Dead Valley below."

"What of an aerial approach?" asked Toko.

"Umbra Castle has many guardians. Winged, nocturnal, dead, alive. I must advance this way, and this way only."

"*We* must advance," Mr. Thorne corrected.

"*What*?" Nagato snarled.

Mr. Thorne crossed his arms. "You heard me."

"This is not a debate," Nagato groused.

"You may need support," said Mr. Thorne. "No plan is foolproof."

"*I'm* foolproof."

"Uma, the great, great, great granddaughter of Ursa, is the reason my father's dead. I must understand why. Even if the journey delivers my fate."

"The High East is infested with wicked creatures. It is an infertile, ash and smoke-laden wasteland. There is no room for tourists!"

"I'm coming as well," Toko said.

"*You*?" Nagato sneered. "What can you—"

Before Nagato finished, there were *thirty* Tokos in the Assembly Room—replicants, all armed with gleaming swords. "I can do plenty, Shadow Bender," said the main one.

"I will not be a shepherd. I don't need back-up." The veins in Nagato's neck bulged.

"Seems we've hit a snag then," Reese said lightly.

Nagato rolled his eyes and pointed at Honor. "You there, servant girl. Bring me that rack of elk. I'm hungry."

Honor went scarlet.

"Hello?" Nagato said. "Servant girl. Did you hear me?"

She clenched her fists. "My name is Honor, and I'm not a servant! If you want something, apologize and say please." She spun and scowled.

Nagato snorted, fetched the platter, and ripped a chunk of meat off with his teeth. "I need passage to Enopolis," he said, smacking. "I assume you have means."

"An unregistered pod is hidden in an electrical room four blocks from Enopolis Radio Tower." Mr. Thorne motioned toward the map. "From there we can—" But he stopped, for a warning gong rang out. Mr. Thorne rushed to the window and peered into the bay. "Warships!" He locked eyes with Reese. "The ceremony..."

Reese nodded. "I've been ill at ease since the tornado this morning."

The Assembly Room emptied to the top deck of the fort. Four bowriders had departed from a vast monitor ship near Cape Nautic's port and were zipping across the bay.

"Spectoculars." Mr. Thorne ordered to a guard. He set the spectoculars against his face and analyzed. "Alright. Hostile Fuzz officers in three bowriders and... agents from The Governor's Office with caustic cannons." He adjusted the dials and surveyed farther out. "On the monitor ship... is... oh no..."

"What?" asked Reese.

"General Zoon..."

"Who?" Jett whispered to Horace.

"Pop's boss's boss," Horace murmured. "The Head of the Intelligence Service."

The bowriders slowed near the Isle's rocky coast. A patriarchal, mole-like Fuzz officer wearing a bright blue uniform leapt up with a megaphone. "Iconoclasts." His voice was high and screechy. "Surrender yourselves. I repeat, surrender yourselves and we will deescalate!"

"Always misplaced his confidence, that one," said Reese.

"We have you surrounded," Captain Fuzz went on. "All of you are charged with detonating the Poltergeist Bomb in Cape Nautic, failing to submit yourselves to Governor Ness's audit, flagrant dissention to Pararealmian law, and the kidnapping of Riley Schrödinger. Wave a white flag, or we will fire!"

Crackling, blue electricity surged from Mr. Thorne's hands, zipped across the water, and smoked Captain Fuzz's megaphone.

"Whooooooa," gasped Jett.

"Awesome," Horace said.

"Norman," Reese shouted. "Diplomacy! We've got to—"

His words were drowned by the guzzling explosion of the caustic cannons. Ectoplasmic bursts began eating through a previously invisible barrier around the Isle. The Iconoclasts readied. "You three," Reese commanded Jett, Horace, and Honor. "To the barracks."

Jett didn't argue. He raced with Horace or Honor downstairs as a clattering resounded throughout the fort. The Isle's foundation quaked.

"We're goners," Horace cried, entering the barracks.

"What do we do?" asked Jett.

A contemptuous laugh came. Shadows unbent and spread across the floor. Nagato strutted out from the murky corner. "I don't have time for this," he growled. "One of you. Operate this 'teleportation pod' so I can get to Enopolis and carry out my mission."

"You're supposed to wait for Mr. Thorne and Toko," Honor reminded.

"The Iconoclasts have asked a favor of me," Nagato parried. "And a big one at that. I order you: beam me to Enopolis!"

"We're not helping you desert us!" Jett declared.

Nagato smirked. "Fine. Stay here and be imprisoned." He headed for the exit, but Toko burst in.

"There's a concussive missile on the monitor ship! All of you, get your things. We're leaving!" The trio snatched their belongings and followed Toko and Nagato back into the courtyard. The noise was so loud now that Jett had to clamp his ears. Stones shattered. Turrets shook. The group found Mr. Thorne in the teleportation pod chamber, calibrating the controls of the secret pod.

"*Something happened*," he shouted. "Most of my pods are disabled!"

"How?" Toko called back.

A detonation deep in the fort. A turret exploded and collapsed. Mr. Thorne shoved the group in, punched a plethora of buttons as if overriding the controls, and boarded. The pod rumbled and, with a hard flash of light, the group fled.

11. Zegna Town

The pod door clanged as Mr. Thorne thrust it open and led the party—Jett, Horace, Honor, Toko, and Nagato—into a corroded bunker. Artificial light strips blinked about the ceiling. Worn martial lockers lined the walls. The quiet of the bunker was enormous, a stark contrast to the calamity at the Isle.

"Where'd you send us?" Honor probed.

"Far." Mr. Thorne slammed the pod door shut. "We must now assume that the Isle will be overtaken." He electrocuted the control panel so no one could follow. "Four unregistered pods exist outside my family estates. All tucked in furtive bases, like the Isle and the one in Enopolis.

We stand in Melee Hill, a relic of the Great War constructed to fend off the Greymarch Army."

"Melee Hill is *where exactly*?" Horace asked.

"The Bocage. Not far from Zegna Town, somewhere few would expect us to go."

"Zegna Town?" Nagato growled. "The High East is *all the way* across the Sasqi Mountains. You've driven us way off course."

"I get that," Mr. Thorne said grimly.

"But *why* were the other pods disabled?" asked Jett.

"Obviously the Iconoclasts have a traitor." Nagato glared at Mr. Thorne and Toko. "You've selected your constituents carelessly."

"How would *you* know?" Honor snapped. "You have—"

"—infallible judgment and intuition," Nagato broke in.

"We must stop bickering," said Toko. "It *is* possible Governor Ness gained leverage over one of us."

Jett adjusted the ifrit horn. Mr. Thorne extracted a parascouter.

"Thorne, how do you expect us to get to Umbra Castle?" Nagato pried. "You've marred our plan. And we have the burden of *these* three now."

"We aren't a burden," Honor snapped.

"It was here or the Drakenbergs. Instead of blaming circumstance, let us focus on the solution from this new vantage." Mr. Thorne led the Party to the bunker's command center, which held panoramic views of the Bocage, a sweeping grassland bordered by woods made of needle-thin, white-barked trees with clumps of artichoke foliage.

"Who else knows about this Melee Hill pod?" asked Nagato.

"Only Reese," answered Mr. Thorne. "And I'd entrust my life with him."

"How touching," Nagato said. "But every man will sing his darkest secret with the right amount of agony."

"Is there anyway the Iconoclasts can withstand General Zoon?" Jett asked.

"Reese is a formidable levilock. I've faith." Mr. Thorne pushed open the rusted bunker door. "Prepare yourselves, everyone. A long road lies ahead of us."

"Filled with danger at every turn?" asked Horace.

The Party proceeded out to a hill of chest-high grass, then down to a wide plain.

"What's a levilock?" Jett asked, parting the grass.

"Reese can create weapons out of light," Honor replied.

"Oh, *man*!"

Jett paused, fingered his windgun. "What, Horace? What d'you see?"

Horace raised a hand against the suns. "I forgot my sunglasses. It's so bright out."

"Twerp," Nagato hissed. "Keep quiet."

"I wonder what else I've forgotten..." Horace mumbled.

"QUIET."

The party marched through the high grass for hours, startling a pack of spindlehorns, which cantered away, and observing turals glide overhead. Otherwise, they were absorbed in thought. The tall grass ended at the edge of the disparate wood.

"No scorpionshoods in here, yeah?" asked Horace.

"Correct," said Toko. "Though that doesn't mean there aren't hazards."

"What's in Zegna Town?" Jett asked Mr. Thorne.

"Magnus Rime. We met once in Focal City. I tried to sell him and his people a teleportation pod. Didn't bite."

The party traversed through the woods for some time, hearing little save Horace's grumblings and the soft clucking of birds. A little while later, a groan came, followed by a tremor.

"Run," Horace cried.

"Shhhh—" Toko grabbed Horace by the collar. "This way."

The party moved toward a cluster of shrubs close to where the sound came. Jett knelt and parted one. A shaggy, blonde rhinoceros with a bowed horn was lying in a glade, breathing heavily. "A karkadann," Toko exclaimed and leapt over the shrubs.

The karkadann was too weak to rise. Toko eased over and caressed its head. "It's alright girl," she said, examining the animal. "Let's see what's wrong." Jett hopped over the shrubs as well. "Careful," Toko warned. "Don't get gored by her horn."

Jett rounded the karkadann at a wide distance and saw Toko evaluating a sharp log jammed in her belly. She glanced at Mr. Thorne. "Tree sap or honey, and a large leaf." Mr. Thorne spun and trotted deep into the trees. "This will hurt," Toko consoled the karkadann. "But you'll feel better when we're done."

"I didn't sign up for animal rescue," Nagato barked. "I told you: we operate at my speed. Let's go."

"If you know the path over the Sasqis, feel free," said Toko.

"Well. I." Nagato shifted his kusarigama blades. "Hurry up, then."

Jett knelt. "How d'you think this happened?"

"Maybe she was running and tripped?" Honor hypothesized.

Horace waddled to a tree and began peeing.

"Poachers trade karkadann horn for exorbitant prices." Toko inspected the karkadann's despondent eyes. "Her pupils aren't dilated. Unlikely she ate something poisonous and fell. I reckon she was spooked."

Mr. Thorne soared over the shrubs with a cordate leaf covered in a sticky brown secretion. "Almost took a sting from traveler bees, so I opted for hangtree sap."

Toko stood, rubbed the karkadann's belly, and planted her feet in the soil by its stomach. "One—" she took a deep breath "—two—three—" she yanked out the log with all her might. The karkadann howled so loud birds took flight from dozens of trees!

"This was in deeper than I thought—" Toko passed the log (covered in sapphire blood) to Honor "—we don't want to leave this. A predator might smell it. She'll need time to regain her strength and find her shelter."

"Great," moaned Horace. "Now the predator will come for us!"

Toko took the sappy leaf and sealed the karkadann's puncture. The karkadann murmured something sweet and, with a few breaths, stood and moseyed off. By the time the karkadann was at the edge of the party's sight, she had reached a springy trot. The Party kept on.

***

A row of cherry laurels marked the end of the woods. Toko had buried the bloody karkadann log deep in mulch, far from the wounded creature. The Party clawed through the cherry laurels into a magnificent orchard. "Where're we now?" Horace asked Mr. Thorne, who was studying the parascouter.

"Yee. Whuddya think yer doin'?" Jett looked at the party. Everyone was confused. "I said—" a voice trilled "—whuddya think yerrr doin'!" A tiny, bedraggled gnome in suspenders and a workshirt was sticking out of the orchard dirt. "Any of you's planning on answering?"

"Look at the lil' pipsqueak," laughed Horace.

The gnome packed soil in its palm and slung it in Horace's face. Honor cackled.

"Hey," Horace shouted, wiping the dirt off. "Why you—"

Toko held Horace back. The gnome puffed out its chest proudly.

Honor crouched. "We didn't mean to intrude, sir. We're heading to Zegna Town."

"Well you ain't there, is you? You're in the orchard of Gardener Pike!"

"By accident," Honor repeated. "I'm not sure you're listening. Could you please point us in the right direction?"

"'Course I could," the gnome peeped. "But why should I?"

"Don't you want us off your orchard?"

"Thorne, consult your parascouter," Nagato directed. "I'm sick of this puny thing." The gnome threw soil at Nagato. His face darkened. "Do that again, and I'll uproot you." His kusarigamas flashed against the sunlight.

The gnome's eyes widened. "Alright, alright. Hold your horses, yous." It straightened its little suspenders and motioned down the orchard.

"Take the lawn east. Trail's there. And don't besmirch our topsoil on the way out!" It popped back in its hole and hurriedly covered it up.

The Party exited Gardener Pike's place onto an earthy footpath which rose in great, curving slopes up the alpine terrain. The air cooled, and before long the bulwarks and billowing chimneys of Zegna Town appeared. Mr. Thorne stopped far from the gate. "Conceal your weapons, everyone. Toko, Honor, boys, stay here. Nagato, you're with me." A pair of crossbows aimed at Mr. Thorne and Nagato as they approached the gate.

"State your names and business," a guard ordered.

"We are mere travelers on the road," Mr. Thorne called back. "We seek shelter and guidance on the journey ahead. Our intention is to stay one night and pay for every service rendered."

"Your path is to where?" asked the other guard.

"We seek to aggress the Sasqi Mountains."

The guards broke out laughing, their crossbows wobbling in their arms.

"Our quest does not concern you," Nagato contended. "Zegna Town is but a brief stop."

The guards' laughter quelled. "You claim to have money. Show us."

Mr. Thorne rummaged through his eggplant topcoat, fetched a silk pouch, and launched it at the gate. Astounded, the guards nearly fell trying to catch it. One opened it, looked pleased, and called down, "What are your names?" Mr. Thorne listed aliases for the party. The guards turned away and conferred. "Very well. You've permission to stay in Zegna Town one night. Our authorities will see to it you are gone by then."

A deep groan came as the gate opened, exposing the old agrarian town with thatched roofs and slop for streets. Jingling carts and folk in ragged cloaks ambled about. The guards nicked a few elecoin from Mr. Thorne's pouch and tossed it down as the party took the main thoroughfare to a canal lined with sheets of ice and berms packed with antiquated shops. A mill with a water wheel bookended one side, and rising high above the entire street was a burnt bell tower so dilapidated it looked like a burst of wind could knock it down.

Nagato returned to the party after parleying with a blacksmith. "Dreggs Inn's over here. A place we can stay."

The party headed for an old-timey brown and white lodge a few blocks over. The door chimed as they entered. In the lobby, a fire crackled near the monocled manager. "Welcome," he greeted, raising his arms. "To Dreggs Inn. To whom do we owe the pleasure?"

"Hi." Toko approached. "We've six. Have a room that fits?"

The manager surveyed the party then asked Jett, "These are your parents?"

"Our guardians," he said, vague.

The manager rubbed his chin. "So you're safe?"

"Well... we trust them. They haven't kidnapped us, if that's what you mean."

"Hmmm. Typically we limit four guests per door. I suppose the Station Suite could suit if we brought in cots." The manager paused. "Although..."

"What?" Mr. Thorne probed.

"The cappuccino machine is broken..."

Mr. Thorne went red. "So!"

"Well, if you can manage without it... it's two hundred elecoin per evening."

Mr. Thorne thumbed out the proper allotment. The manager passed over a hefty brass key. "Third floor, second door. Stairs to the right.

If you do need a cappuccino, Beebarb's Haus is the place, two lanes down the canal."

Mr. Thorne adjusted his circular glasses. "We don't need cappuccinos!"

Jett laughed. So did Honor and Toko.

Horace, preoccupied, inquired, "Where's food?"

"D'you ever stop eating?" asked Honor.

"Leave me alone!"

"Ah, Morrow Tavern's," the manager explained. "Delectable mastodon ribs. Consider visiting the hot springs up the slope due west of the Charred Tower while in Zegna Town. Wonderful on a frosty morning, if I may say."

"One more thing," said Mr. Thorne. "Where might we find Magnus Rime?"

"Oh." The manager wiped a smudge off the counter with a rag. "Magnus is away, hunting a baku. No one will be able to tell you when Magnus and his riders will be back."

Honor stiffened. "A baku's nearby?"

"Seems one makes its way close to Zegna Town every few years." The manager gestured up the hill. "Stop by the Rime's stables if you desire more information. Up the slope, take a left. You'll see the grounds after a short hike."

"Stables?" Jett asked.

But a couple entered the lobby and attracted the manager's attention. The Party exited Dreggs Inn and roamed north on the canal.

"A baku near Zegna Town. A gargaunt in the Alluvial Lands," Honor said, exasperated. "Something's off in the wild."

"Beasts stray more than you'd think," Nagato said.

"Someone mind explaining what baku are?" Jett asked.

"Steel-blue elephants with serrated tusks," said Horace. "Baku feed on people's dreams and turn them to nightmares."

The party ventured up a cabin-lined slope then took a fork left onto a road of prominent chalets. An ornate fence and stable were nestled on the last plot, with a straggling estate perched back in the acreage. The party crossed a muddy paddock into the stable and paused in the aisle amid the smell of manure and straw and loud smatterings.

"The stalls are ginormous," Jett said.

"That's because they house silverhoofed longma." A stall opened. A pyknic woman with charcoal hair tromped out with a sudsy bucket. "Strapping creatures, longma are. Wicked strong and lightning quick, with keener minds than you'd think."

"Dragon horses?" Horace was amazed. "I've always wanted to see one." He raced to a stall and climbed the railing. "Jett, check it out!"

Jett hustled over and did the same. Inside the stall was a pewter-gray, scaled horse with a spiked tail, pumpkin-colored mane, and creamy eyes munching on a hunk of raw meat. Smoke poured from its flaring nostrils as it tore apart the sinews.

"I thought they had wings?" Horace asked.

The longma glanced over and neighed; only the neigh sounded like a soothing flute. Jett turned to Horace, brow furrowed. They started laughing.

"Are you the stablemaster?" Mr. Thorne asked the woman as the boys dropped down.

She dropped the bucket and wiped her forehead with a dirty sleeve. "Nina Rime. Something I can help you with, since you wandered onto my property?"

"I apologize, we were told to come here. Your son and I are acquainted. I know Magnus to be an argute, honest man, whom I've nothing but respect for. We need his help to cross the Sasqis."

Nina cocked an eyebrow. "Why in the world'd ya wanna do that?"

"It's probably best if I don't say."

"Well, I'll save you a conversation. Magnus won't accompany you. Only fools attempt the Sasqis. *Fools*."

"It's not a tourist expedition," Nagato grumbled. "Our business is urgent. Navigating around the Sasqis would take weeks."

"But you'd make it alive."

"The risk is ours to take. We're only asking for Magnus's knowledge of the terrain."

Nina shrugged. "He's out on a baku hunt. You'll have to wait."

"Any idea how long?" Toko inquired.

Nina adjusted a harness hanging on a stall. "Baku hunts are unpredictable. Magnus and his crew left four days ago, up to you to guess."

"Ms. Rime, do you know the path across the Sasqis?" Jett asked.

Nina finished latching the harness. "Sure, that's simple. Inkprickle Pass lies just beyond the Obsidian Gate. Take it to the foot of the Sasqis then decide how you want to die: treading through the snow or venturing below it."

"Surely *some* head up the slopes now and then?" Honor asked.

"To the absolute lowest parts, sure, but only when required." Nina ambled to the mound of hulking meat atop a fridge and wrestled another piece onto her shoulder.

"Caring for the longmas must be hard," said Jett.

"Well it ain't duck soup!" Nina doddered to a different stall and heaved the meat over the railing. "Don't mean to be trite, but I'm only telling you what my son will. Magnus is President of the Broken Arrow Hunting Lodge. He's seen more of the north than anyone in Zegna Town and he dreads riding anywhere near them Sasqis." She hacked up mucus and spit it in the muck. "If you're determined to go, drop into Olaf's Outfitters for fur coats. Otherwise, you'll freeze into popsicles the first night."

The party thanked Nina for her time and departed. Dusk fell as they headed for Morrow Tavern, a few streets south of Dreggs Inn. The night air chilled the alpine village. Morrow Tavern was snug and clement, however. A chandelier with a hundred candles hung over the patrons drinking ale from the communal flagon. Some swayed and sung dulcet songs near oboes and fiddles. The party meandered to the calmest section and, before long, their shedua-wood table was piled with honeycomb rolls, wolverine soup, mastodon ribs, curried mutton, cacao pudding, and lotus leaf tea.

"It isn't fair what's been done to you three," Mr. Thorne said later. "But beyond the Obsidian Gate lie dangers far worse than prison. Death will constantly be in our face." He and Toko exchanged a look. "We think it's best you three remain here in Zegna Town. I'll convince Magnus to grant you leave."

"Won't news of the Isle reach Zegna Town eventually?" Jett asked.

"You'll have Magnus's protection and your aliases. The people here are not fond of Focal City and outside authorities. You'd be safer than the Sasqis and High East."

"So you're just going to leave us?" Honor asked.

Horace shoveled cacao pudding into his jowls. "That's alright with me."

Mr. Thorne fretted. "It was irresponsible to involve you in the first place."

"It wasn't your fault," Jett said. "You had to act accordingly. There was nil time to think."

"Goodness. Could it be?" The party looked up from their plates. A dingy man with a mullet and eyes fit for an alpaca staggered over with a tankard. "The boy wonder, Norman Thorne, in Morrow Tavern? I must be dreaming." The noise ceased. The crowd turned. "Name's Crenkshaw. Me aunt and uncle worked in the Dowse Town PsyMart for years."

The noise resumed, patrons returning to their activities.

Crenkshaw fell into the empty seat as a waitress passed by with a pitcher. Crenkshaw raised his tankard. The waitress poured. "Bit more." He winked as the ale foamed to the brim. "That's the ticket then!" The waitress sauntered off. "Haven't heard mention of a Thorne since yer daddy and Uma slayed ole Ruth Schrödinger," Crenkshaw croaked.

"How dare you!" snapped Toko.

Jett saw Mr. Thorne trying to remain civil.

"*The Gulog* murdered Ruth," Honor rebuked. "We've proof."

Crenkshaw hiccupped. "I don't believe you."

"Well you're an idiot."

"Ha. I bet all you've got is drivel."

"*You're* drivel."

Crenkshaw leaned closer, his eyes popped with disbelief, breath stinking. "You mean to tell me you think Gene Thorne and Uma Umbra summoned the Gulog, the Baron of the High

East... the audacious, unsparing, lich leader of the Greymarch Army after he was burned to a crisp following the Great War? And that the Gulog then killed Ruth and escaped to another world without a trace? It was all a fabrication to Gene get off!"

"Uma is a *netherwitch*," Honor refuted. "Necromancy, bewitching, mind control, it's what she does!"

"What she *did*, you mean." The party said nothing. Crenkshaw scoffed, took a swig. "So, whatchu all in town for?"

"Leave us, you wastrel," Nagato thundered. "Unless you want to sleep in a coffin tonight."

Crenkshaw snatched his tankard. "So much for good company." He wandered away.

Marrow Tavern growing rowdier, the party wrapped their meal and departed for Dreggs Inn, where they settled into the Station Suite, which had two agreeable beds, a fireplace (already lit), oversized armchairs, and a pair of cots.

"Thorne, is this cosseted enough for you?" Nagato mocked. "Think you'll manage?"

Jett, Horace, and Honor removed their bastioarmor tunics, windguns, and the ifrit horn, and piled under the covers of one bed (Horace in the middle). Toko and Mr. Thorne sat against the pillows on the other but didn't lay their heads. Nagato flunked into an armchair near the fire. And slowly, Jett drifted asleep.

12. THE BROKEN ARROW LODGE

A black sky on a surreal, moonless night. Jett trundled across a tor holding a lantern, swinging wildly, in the shimmering fog around him. Something was coming.

"No, no, no," he gasped. "Please. Not me."

"HE-HEHE-HE-HEHE."

Jett raced up stone steps toward a tunnel and twisted back for a quick glance.

"HE-HEHE-HE-HEHE." The ghoulish cackle reverberated along the tunnel walls. The shimmering fog thickened as Jett darted around a turn, the lantern lifting in his hand from inertia. A fly zipped by the light. Jett stopped. The temperature skyrocketed.

"HE-HEHE-HE-HEHE! Nowhere to go." The Gulog slinked through the fog. "'Allo, Jett." It reached for him and—

Jett shot upright in bed, doused in sweat. A cold breeze rustled the curtains to his left in the Station Suite. The fire was dim. Something short and wiry was creeping in front of it. Starlight glimmered against a knife. "Mr. Thorne, MR. THORNE!"

Mr. Thorne sprung awake as the creature leapt on him and slashed at him with its blade. He caught it by the wrist and threw the creature down. It darted to the window and vaulted out. A shadow swept after it.

"Norman! Are you hurt?" Toko hit the lights.

Mr. Thorne fished for his circular eyeglasses and assessed himself. "I... think I'm fine."

Toko looked at Jett. "What did you see?"

He felt terribly, terribly weak. "I... saw... a small thing carrying a knife."

The shadow skidded back in with a crash. The darkness slipped down and spread across the stone floor. "Redcap, explain yourself!"

Nagato bayed, a kusarigama blade against the creature's repellant face.

The redcap had mottled skin, stringy hair and prominent teeth that protruded from its lips. It spit on the ground. Nagato ran the blade along its stomach, cutting it. The redcap squealed miserably. "The next one ends your life!"

"A bounty on their heads!" The redcap pointed at Mr. Thorne and Toko. "Traitorous plotters! Treason against the Governor."

"The Governor sent you?" Toko demanded.

The redcap squirmed.

Nagato raised his kusarigama. "Who issued the bounty, runt?" He set the blade against its temple. "Tell us and you'll see daylight."

"Mesmer!" it cried.

"Zoon?" Blood rushed from Toko's face. "Governor Ness's special advisor?"

Nagato shook the redcap. It nodded.

"How did word of the bounty find you?" Mr. Thorne interrogated.

"Word spreads."

Nagato sent a kusarigama through the redcap's head. Blood splattered against the wall. "I'll fetch the manager and convene the Zegna Town guards. Watch yourselves." Nagato let the corpse fall to the floor. He wiped his blade casually.

"Why'd you do that?" Honor yelled.

"The operations of bounty networks are irrelevant." Nagato stormed out, leaving the party in mirthless silence.

Jett glanced around, utterly daunted. Toko was pacing. Mr. Thorne had gone ashen and was leaning forward on the mattress. Honor and Horace were shaking.

"You look sick." Toko approached Jett and brushed hair from his face.

"I had this... dream." He tried to recall it, but his energy was sapped. "Only... it wasn't a dream. It felt like it was actually happening. The Gulog was... chasing me. I was alone and running, and it caught me."

"The baku," Honor suggested.

"It very well may have fed on you tonight," Toko said. "We'll get you food."

"Then Magnus hasn't finished the hunt." Mr. Thorne rose and pottered over. "Jett, thank you. You saved my life."

Jett managed to grin. "Just returning the favor."

"Man, I *can't wait* to see what's next," Horace said in jest.

A throng of Zegna Town guards and Dreggs Inn's manager entered with Nagato. "Dear, dear," the manager said, shuffling around the body. "How ghastly."

The head guard faced her report. "Put out word: a redcap from the Southern Shrublands has snuck into Zegna Town. There could be other illicit visitors around." The report exited. The head guard addressed others. "Cover the body. Carry it out." She studied the party. "I suppose you needed to kill it?"

"Yes," said Nagato.

"Shame. Interrogation may have unlocked answers. Anyway, I suggest you relocate."

"We're fine," Nagato stated. "We won't let our vigilance wither again."

The head guard spotted the windguns. "I don't remember permits clearing authorization?"

Mr. Thorne rubbed his neck. "Can't be too careful. Don't you reckon?"

Guards laid a sheet over the bloody body and began to remove it from the Station Suite. The head guard took this in as the manager began mopping. "I understand you've business with Magnus Rime?" the head guard asked.

"He's a friend," Mr. Thorne said. "We intend to stay in Zegna Town only long enough to speak with him. Is that alright?"

The manager finished cleaning and leaned on the mop. "Anything I can get you all? Warm ox milk? Cleese Chocolate from Enopolis?"

"Cleese's," Horace said. "Definitely."

"Nagato informed me of your errand," said the head guard. "You may stay in Zegna Town until Magnus returns, but no longer. Lock the windows and door. We'll keep additional eyes out about town." She receded into the hall with the manager, who, as the door closed, muttered, "I sure hope this doesn't affect their review."

Mr. Thorne locked the door. "I'm afraid it can no longer be avoided. You three will have to join us beyond the Obsidian Gate."

Jett's heart skipped.

Mr. Thorne shook his head, frustrated. "Morrow Tavern... wandering the canal freely... we should have been more prudent, more reclusive."

Toko wrenched the hangings shut and fluffed the trio's comforter. "For now, everything's fine. You three get some sleep." She headed across the room and flicked off the lights.

Horace snored immediately. Honor seemed to drift soon after. But Jett was too adrenalized to rest. He slipped from bed and took the recliner beside Nagato at the fire. Mr. Thorne and Toko were in the other bed, eyes closed, though Jett sensed they were alert. "I'm scared," he admitted. "We're being attacked from every direction."

Nagato stared into the flames, ruminating. "I used to train in the foothills outside Asija Village. I'd venture into the wilderness and become ensconced in nature's harmony. The world outside would disappear as I'd endeavor for enlightenment. As the Great War approached, the peace of the foothills waned. Nature herself changed. The air grew weighted and aggrieved. Sorrow flowed through the flowers and trees." Nagato cast his eyes deep into Jett's for the first time. There was profound power in them. "I feel that heaviness today."

"That's why you fight with us?"

"That harmonic imbalance drives my ferocity, yes. My loyalty to what is right."

Jett decided to ask a question which had been fixed in his mind. "Do you remember anything... from the afterlife?"

"Nothing," said Nagato. "But that's not what is bothering me. Prince Icarus betrayed me. I can't stop thinking that his malice didn't end there. I must learn what happened to my family."

Jett placed a hand on Nagato's shoulder. "If it helps, I miss my family as well. Like you, I've been brought into an unfamiliar place." He climbed back into bed. Eventually, his mind grew tired enough to rest.

***

"Alright you three," Toko said in the early morning. "Up and at 'em."

Jett gazed at the drool on his pillow. Horace grunted next to him and curled the covers tighter. The bedspring creaked as Honor clambered to her feet. Outside, the suns threw a silvery tint over Zegna Town. Rain was looming.

"Jett, Horace," Toko repeated. "Rise and shine. You're an example setter, Honor."

Jett stretched and set his feet on the chilly stone. Mr. Thorne and Nagato, of course, were dressed and wide awake.

"Uggh. What're we supposed to do?" Horace said. "Magnus isn't back yet."

"How about finding out what happened to Mom and Pop?" Honor scorned. "Or the Iconoclasts? Or have you forgotten all that's happened?"

Horace yawned. "But I thought we shouldn't be seen about town?"

"We need to make preparations," Toko said. "The Sasqi Mountains are harsh at best. Non-perishable food, drinking water, packs, garb, all things we hadn't prepared for."

"Horace—" Nagato rapped his fingers against a wooden table "—if you don't get out of bed... I'm going to drench you with an ice bucket."

The party was soon ready to depart. Mr. Thorne unlocked the door. "What's this?" He lifted a note atop a tray of steaming cups on the hall floor. "Fresh cappuccinos," Mr. Thorne read aloud. "The least I could do." He groaned. "How thick is this manager?" He brought the tray in and dolled out cups. Jett and Horace declined. "My." Mr. Thorne licked foam from his lips. "These are good." The boys snickered.

The party left Dreggs Inn for Olaf's Outfitters. Navigating the canal, it was instantly clear that word of the redcap entry had gotten out. Every cluster of people along the waterway was in deep conversation about it, murmuring with concerned looks, glancing around like they may be attacked at any second. Bulletins were pinned on corners and in shop windows, warning citizens to be wary of trespassers of every sort.

By midmorning, Olaf had the party fitted in saber-tooth tiger overcoats with matching gloves and caps, courtesy of Mr. Thorne. As they left, a terrible sleet commenced, driving the party into Ajax's Café, where they gobbled sausage-gravy and barley bread, apple turnovers, and creamed beef, and learned from the waitress that *The Focal City Fanzine* ran a day late all the way out in Zegna Town.

Post brunch, the sleet didn't abate, so the party tossed their overcoats over their heads and flitted through the icy rills back to Dreggs Inn, where they stayed for the remainder of the day. Everyone except Nagato fell asleep to the coziness of firelight that evening.

The sleet was gone the following day, and news that the riders of the Broken Arrow Lodge had returned brought fresh life to the party.

"Magnus is sensible and august, but cavalier," Mr. Thorne told the party on the way to the Charred Tower. "So taper your tempers... Nagato..."

The lobby was constructed with rose marble, surprisingly, and held an aura of imminence, opposite its dilapidated exterior.

"Norman Thorne here to see Magnus Rime," Mr. Thorne told the prim clerk.

She frowned. "I'm sorry, sir, but Magnus is unavailable. It was a treacherous hunt, as you no doubt heard."

"Magnus and I are old friends."

"I can't permit you to see Magnus," the clerk said, firm. "Perhaps come back tomorrow."

"Just get him! Will you?" Mr. Thorne barked.

"So much for tapering tempers," muttered Nagato.

The clerk glowered and reached for the paraphone. "Yes... Magnus Rime, please." The clerk stared daggers at Mr. Throne while she waited. "Hi, Magnus. Yes, there's a Mr. Corn here to see you—"

"—Mr. *Thorne*."

"A Mr. Thorne... yes... he's with... one, two, three, four, five others... yes... yes... alright." She hung up and gestured at the elevator. "Wait there. Magnus is coming down."

The elevator soon dinged, and out strolled a stalwart hunter in stirrups and riding boots. Magnus's kingly face was unshaven and begrimed. "Well, well," he drawled with a vibrant smile. "I heard the noble aristocrat Norman Thorne was in Zegna Town. Though, I admit, I didn't believe it."

Mr. Thorne bowed. "I owe you an explanation. But perhaps we could discuss it privately."

Magnus examined the party. Discord bloomed in his eyes. "Who's after you?"

"May we please talk in quiet?"

With a deferential nod, Magnus escorted the party into the lift. The elevator climbed, opened, and Magnus led them through the towering, antler-handled doors of the Broken Arrow Lodge. Mounts of beasts—minotaur, ammit, manticore, fenrir, more—lined the high-ceilinged lounge and floors. Wood-iron tables and bars, leatherbound sofas, and massive mantles filled the room too. In the back, the bedraggled riders were knocking tankards around the steel-blue head of the baku, lying on a tarp. The baku's serrated tusks jutted upwards in sharp, cruel twists. Jett was unnerved, considering how the orphic creature had fed on his thoughts and dreams.

"She was deep in Lycan Valley, in a nasty dwelling," Magnus said proudly. "Had to fend off a pack of vaewolves before we found her."

"I don't understand..." Honor gazed out the window over Zegna Town. "How is the Charred Tower intact? It looks like it's about to collapse."

Magnus chuckled. "Oh, we replace a brick here and there every now and then. But I assure you, the fundamental structure is sound."

"What happened though?" asked Horace.

"One spring morning years back, that scaled the Obsidian Gate—" Magnus gestured above the Broken Arrow Lodge crest, where the head of a grizzly bear fifteen times the size of any grizzly Jett had ever seen was mounted "—we don't know its name, but that was no bear. It was a *demon* that spit fire like a flamethrower. Many were killed fighting it. Half of Zegna Town was turned to fiery rubble. From the roof of *this* very tower, my grandfather conjured an icicle storm which smote the demon, but not before the tower was scorched." Magnus motioned around the lounge with resignation. "The Broken Arrow Lodge dates back centuries. The stories of many accredited hunters live here, many fallen brethren." He pointed at Jett's ifrit horn. "It seems you've a tale of your own there?"

Jett glanced at Mr. Thorne, who nodded permission. And so, as Jett had done multiple times already, he rehashed his and the party's miraculous story in detail. Magnus rubbed his dirty face after. "An Earthling and the legendary Shadow Bender stand before me. Numinous, truly. If you all are correct in that Uma Umbra is again active, you have my aid." He considered something. "It's possible this explains gradual changes my riders and I have noticed in the wild. There has been a... quiet turbulence beyond the Obsidian Gate, though we had attributed it to the baku."

"What exactly have you seen?" said Nagato.

"Beasts migrating prematurely, encroaching on our well-tilled hunting ground. It's not that they're making a push, per se; more that they appear to have been forced out by something." Magnus caressed his stubble then strode to an arching windowpane and gestured far out into the sundering whitecaps. "To make the trek, you must reach Sabina's Saddle on night one. By noon the next day, you need to scale Arête Peak and descend the northeastern slopes by nightfall or you'll freeze. From there, you cross the desolate Spurned Cliffs which border the High East." Magnus looked intently upon the party. "I will bear as much of this burden as I can. But my ultimate concern is my people. My top riders and I will prepare your packs and take you up Inkprickle Pass tomorrow. All I can offer from there is a warm meal if you return. Go now and rest. Meet us at the Obsidian Gate at dawn."

"Thank you, Magnus," Jett said, echoed by Toko and Honor.

"There is something else."

Magnus beheld Mr. Thorne.

"There was a battle in the Diluvian Sea on an island. If there is a way to gather intelligence without kicking up notice... we'd greatly appreciate an update."

Magnus nodded. "I'll do my best."

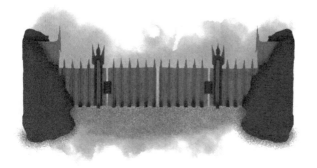

13. THROUGH THE OBSIDIAN GATE

At sunrise, dressed in saber-tooth tiger overcoats, the party checked out of Dreggs Inn and marched to the back of Zegna Town. This morning was colder than the previous two. Atop silverhoofed longmas, Magnus and three other riders stood before the heaping Obsidian Gate, gripping reigns. "You look rested." Magnus tipped his head. "That won't last."

"Any news of the Isle?" Honor asked.

"Word hasn't reached our land yet. At least not in my network." Magnus pointed to the trio.

"You're with Nasra and me. Hop on." Nasra the longma gave a fluty neigh.

Four guards hoisted open the Obsidian Gate, exposing Inkpricle Pass, which zig-zagged like a trough up the rocky, slate terrain toward the Sasqis. Magnus chirruped. The longmas took off. The cold air morphed quickly into an icy breeze.

"I think Nasra's faster than the Silver Pigeon!" Jett told Horace while holding Honor.

"Yeah right."

"Nasra and I grew up as tykes," Magnus called over his shoulder. "My parents gave her to me as a foal. I was riding before I could putter about on my own feet."

The vegetation thinned as the longmas ascended the terrain. The trees turned wiry, and ruins of vast bone appeared around rundown hovels. The troughed Inkprickle Pass shifted into taluses of boulder which then flattened into a muddy plain. Midday, near a gulch with oxbows, the longmas stopped. "This is as far as we take you," Magnus said, the Sasqi Mountains even more enormous so close. Hesitantly, the party dismounted and hoisted the packs on their shoulders. "Lycan Valley is to the west. Cockatrice roam the heaths in the southeast. Don't stray near either. Remember: you must reach

Sabina's Saddle by dusk. Good luck." Magnus turned Nasra back toward Zegna Town, now a blip down the basin, and, with the other riders, took off. In no time, they were out of sight.

Snow crunched under the party's boots when they reached the lowest spur of the Sasqis early that afternoon. Jett's thighs burned. Polar wind nipped at his nose. His eyes were watery. Snow began to fall as the party climbed the next massif. Powder accumulated on their overcoats and caps, and soon rose to their knees. Mr. Thorne, carving a channel in the snow, dictated their pace. Nagato guarded the rear. The world grew disorienting and white.

"This is horrible!" Horace yelled, high up the slopes. "How much farther is Sabina's Saddle?"

Mr. Thorne consulted his parascouter but said nothing. Dusk approached, which brought with it the baying of beasts. The snow grew so thick that Jett could hardly see Mr. Thorne ahead.

"How much farther?" Horace cried out again.

Mr. Thorne paused. "Not much longer. We must press on."

"Somehow I don't believe him," Horace said.

"Shut up, Horace." Honor wiped ice from her nose.

Ceaselessly the party trudged under descending suns, slipping in fresh powder, weakening from exertion until at last a wide ridge appeared at the edge of the snowflakes, bringing with it newfound faith. The party bowed against the raging wind and raced forward, cresting the final knoll only for a horrendous wind to blow them back, but they held strong.

"This is Sabina's Saddle?" Jett asked.

"Wait here," Nagato ordered as Mr. Thorne stowed his parascouter. "Might be deathspinners crawling within." Nagato slipped in as vaewolf howls rang from Lycan Valley below, dampened by the whirring snow.

"I don't care! Let the deathspinners have me!" Horace screamed, shivering, and flooded into the hollow. The rest of the party followed. In minutes, Toko had a fire kindled and Nagato had returned, confirming the hollow's unoccupancy. Jett stooped with Honor and Horace around the flame. His hands, feet, and face thawed as he watched, in a daze, the twirling flames play. Mr. Thorne and Nagato took a second pass to assure the party's safety and were not seen for some time.

"Man, could I go for a woolly mammoth burger from Goosefeather," Horace chirped, scooping blood sausage porridge from a tin-can with his fingers and sniffing it. "This stuff stinks."

"Quiet," Toko urged.

Jett poured a gulp of porridge into his mouth, super hungry. "I don't mind it."

"I hate Uma for making us go through this," Honor complained. "I hate her."

"You and me both," agreed Toko.

Mr. Thorne and Nagato returned as a meteor shower sprinted across the nocturnal sky.

Curled later in his blanket, Jett fell asleep with a semi-full belly and warm face. Nagato, Toko, and Mr. Thorne took turns guarding the hollow and tending to the fire. Horace's snores were often drowned out by the yowls of the beasts of the wild.

***

Smoke wafted into Jett's nose as Nagato stamped out the dwindling fire in the morning. Outside, the snow had grown in fury and was now a swirling blizzard, making Jett wish he was back at Hane cottage or, preferably, his own house.

"No breaks today," Mr. Thorne announced, almost as if trying to convince himself. "Arête Peak by noon, descend by dusk."

"And what if we don't?" asked Horace, waking.

The party nibbled balut eggs and marula fruit frugally then set off, gaining little ground while slogging up steeper and slicker ice. The air thinned. Jett's legs were feeble as the suns rose against the incessant snow.

"*Fine*," Toko said mid-morning, following Horace's fifth request to take a break. "Norman, give us a moment."

Mr. Thorne stared back, eyebrows iced over, face frustrated, clasping his parascouter. "Arête Peak is just to the left," he shouted over the wind. "Beyond this couloir. Then we can—"

A roar up the gorge.

Jett squinted through the snow.

Another roar.

The outline of a humongous, furry, white ape came. It beat its chest and bared its giant teeth. Jett's eyes widened enormously. "YETI." Mr. Thorne turned. "RUN!" The party sprinted away the slope as the yeti barreled around the couloir. "Go, go, go!"

Suddenly, Jett was bulldozed by Horace, who had tripped. He and Horace flew into Honor, who tumbled into Nagato. The group snowballed down the slope, jouncing around and landing painfully on a flat plane.

"*Horace*," Honor screamed, leaping to her feet. "Moron!"

Jett glanced back. The yeti was near the edge of the couloir. Its roar shook the mountain.

"Up!" Nagato seized Horace by his neck as Toko and Mr. Thorne slid athletically down. Mr. Thorne eyed his parascouter.

"There's a tunnel in the mountain."

The party sped to an iced-over, metal door in a cornice. Shockwaves sparked as Mr. Thorne melted the threshold.

"ANY DAY, THORNE." Nagato glanced at the yeti as it leapt off the gorge, roared, and galumphed toward them. Ice chunks broke across the ground.

"Now or never!" Jett howled.

Mr. Thorne grabbed the wheel and spun with all his might. The shaft opened. "Inside!"

The party vaulted in. Mr. Thorne heaved the door closed as the yeti arrived and pounded against it. Its punches resounded in the dark passage, then... a rumble... low and deep. The yeti went quiet. It took off in the other direction. The rumble compounded.

"Avalanche!" Horace shouted.

Heart hammering, Jett listened as the monstrous snow-wave trundled down the mountain, crashing over itself with a godly force until the world outside went still and the darkness of the tunnel enveloped him.

"What do we do?" yelped Honor.

Nagato set a hand on her mouth. "Shhh. We know not what dwells in here with us."

"I don't know where we are," said Mr. Thorne, morose. "But I've a guess." He flicked on the parascouter light and surveyed the map for a long stretch. "The Guildhalls of Dorr, the ancient fastness of the Dorrean tribe."

"What does that mean?" Jett probed.

"It means yet again we've been thrown off course," Nagato said.

"But how do we proceed? Can we?"

"I'll tell you one thing. I'd rather be able to see."

Mr. Thorne ignored this, turned, and led the party on.

Perhaps an hour passed, Jett wasn't sure, perhaps it was more by the time the party emerged in a gloomy room. His eyes had now adjusted to the lack of light. Mr. Thorne passed the parascouter's dim glow over the room, illuminating cobwebbed counters of chipped stone and wooden shelves with decayed bins surrounding a well. "I think it's a kitchen?" Jett whispered.

"Long abdicated," Toko said.

"Horace," Honor muttered.

"What?"

"You're breathing really loud."

"I can't help how I *breathe*, Honor."

Jett gazed in the well at a pool of arctic water. "Should we refill our canteens?"

"The Dorreans were foragers—" Mr. Thorne peered in the well "—they drilled deep into the mountains' aquifers and supplied Pararealm with mineral water, long before modern irrigation. The Greymarch Army drove their way in during the Great War, poisoned the aquifers, blew the groundwork. We shouldn't risk what remains."

A rushing sound grew in the mountain's belly. It sounded like a thundering stampede. Vicious snorts echoed in the tunnels. Jett stopped breathing, gripped his windgun, bracing, but the sounds vanished. "What was that?" He eased.

"Gougers," Toko proposed.

"Mountain hogs," Mr. Thorne concurred. "A welcome sign."

"*Why*?" said Horace.

"It means there's more than one way out," Nagato explained.

"And that the water is safe?" asked Honor.

"Gougers digestive systems are different. Best we not test it."

The party ventured through corridors, up staircases, down stairwells, and along passages for hours without disturbance, following the parascouter. Often, just beyond the parascouter's light, Jett would catch glimpses of jagged offshoots which disappeared quickly into shadows, where he imagined savage things grew.

Evening came (known by the parascouter's time and their bodily clocks), and the party hunkered in a tucked-away chamber deemed safe as any. "No fire tonight," Nagato ordered. "And eat sparingly. We must pass under these mountains unnoticed, and we don't know how long we may be down here."

Jett nodded with unease.

"I hope Mom and Pop are holding up alright," Honor told Horace before asking the party, "What d'you think's happening in Focal City?"

"No point in speculating," Nagato averred.

"It's hard not to though." Honor looked at Mr. Thorne and cleared her throat. "All this time you've been running Thorne Corp., you've also been co-leading the Iconoclasts with Reese... how did you find the time?"

"Liberties are being erased. Atrocities have been swept under the rug. Law-abiding civilians are being locked up. You make time to combat that. If we lose freedom, what do we have?"

Nagato rose suddenly and drew his blades. The party froze. Soon, Jett heard what Nagato did: faint footsteps pattering about, drawing nearer and nearer.

"Evening." The voice was shrill. "Boy, am I glad to run into someone."

"Stop," Nagato hissed. "Name yourself and your business."

A petite, elfin man materialized against the edge of the parascouter light. "I's Rory the Reconnoiter." Rory grinned, displaying a gap in his front teeth.

"Reconnoiter is a wartime title," said Toko.

"Ahh." Rory wagged a finger. "In the markets, the battle never ceases. I's sent here to search for undervalued real estate."

Confused, Jett eyed the party, then asked, "Real estate?"

"Right-o," Rory pepped. "I represent a visionary investor in Enopolis. Sends me all about Pararealm scouting development opportunities."

"But here? Under the Sasqis?"

"Oh, come on now. The Guildhall of Dorr was once a sight to see! Bit of refreshed infrastructure, proper water repurification, fresh lacquer and coats of paint, and we might have a winner." Rory dropped his pack. "Mind if I join yous? I's been traveling alone a fortnight and could use a drop of company."

"How'd you get down here?" Toko asked.

"Redroot Forest. Stairs in the tree with the Dorrean crest. Didn't you do the same?"

The party was quiet.

"I've got me own food," Rory urged. "All I'm asking for is company."

"You're too trusting," Nagato derided.

"And you're too *untrusting*." Rory sat, smiled, and withdrew a long, brown paper baguette bag. "Say," he told Horace. "Have any of 'em sour candidrops?"

"No?"

"How about Cleese's Chocolate?"

"No."

"What kinda kid are you!" Rory wondered. "Kids're always supposed to have candy. Something's awry in the world these days."

"What!"

"Shhhhh," Nagato ordered. "All of you."

"Never mind candy," Toko said. "Rory, how long have you been under the mountains?"

Rory shrugged indifferently and bit into his baguette. "A fortnight. I told you."

"And you're just... okay, roaming around here by yourself?" Jett asked.

"Ain't exactly thrilled about it," Rory chortled and spit ham on Horace's leg. "But I'm half-Fossorian, so can see fine in the dark."

"Eh!" Horace flicked the ham away.

"Suppose I'm docile about it," Rory admitted. "Still. Gots bills to pay back home. And I reckon these halls provide plenty of space to think, dare you consider the silver lining."

"Have you covered most of the underground then?" asked Toko.

"Course not. Passages below the Sasqis never end." Rory raised an eyebrow. "Say, why's you lot down here anyhow?"

"We're heading to the High East," Jett explained.

Rory squealed. "Horrible market. No developments worth a darn or a dime."

"That's not why we're going."

"Anything we ought to be aware of?" Mr. Thorne said. "We heard gougers earlier."

"Only dem snakeheads—" Rory swallowed "—dem slimy amphibian lizards. Deeper you go, more abundant the water, so be mindful." He took another chomp. "So what's in the High East?"

"Business," said Toko.

Rory's eyebrow climbed higher. "A meeting? What kind?"

"With someone we don't like."

"Then why take it?"

"Because we have to."

"That doesn't make much sense."

"We agree," said Honor.

Rory waved his sandwich at her. "You all don't let on much."

The night passed without fire. Jett heard nothing except Rory's unabating pitch to Mr. Thorne about real estate investments and chat on the lore of the Dorreans and the felling of their tribe. Horace didn't snore.

***

For breakfast, Jett and Horace thankfully munched éclairs left by Rory while the rest of the party packed. The path that morning rose and lowered more abruptly than the prior night, and the slew of gurgling water increased. Beginning mid-day, the party, for hours, ascended a switchback staircase and found themselves in a monolithic atrium by early eve. In awe, the sixsome paused and studied what they could of the place.

"The Guildhall of Dorr," Mr. Thorne explained. "Rather, its' remains, defiled by the enemy and gathering dust for centuries." A serene, black lake covered most of the sprawling floor, which was littered with gigantic fallen columns and shattered runes of Dorrean leaders. Mr. Thorne referred to the parascouter then pointed to the opposite end of the Guildhall. "That'll be the exit then!" Across an arching, hairline pass, Jett could see natural light.

With the party, he hurried up the fraying pass, eager for sunshine. One day in the dark was already driving him batty. The hairline pass crested over the Guildhall water and curled around the few still-standing columns. The fresh air Jett could almost taste. The beam of sunshine ahead looked like heaven, but he stopped.

"We'll catch our breath out there," Toko urged, temporarily slowing.

Jett gazed across the tranquil, black lake.

"Snakeheads can't reach us here," she assured him.

"I hear... a sniff."

A ripple rose in the lake and spread. Bubbles sprouted. Water sloshed and seethed as something rose high toward the ceiling. A horrendous gnash came. Jett buckled at the knees.

A finned serpent, with dozens of pale eyes and a sinuous, ridged hide had emerged and noshed Toko. Jett stared at its teeth, long as sabers, as the serpent swallowed Toko and reared up a hundred feet and hissed its' slimy, prehensile tongue. The serpent screeched.

"A tannin..." Mr. Thorne stepped in front of Jett and muttered. "How can this be... ?"

Jett was petrified, shell-shocked. So too were Honor and Horace.

As if endless, the tannin soared higher, and grimaced. Behind his circular glasses, Mr. Thorne's eyes burned bright with blue electricity. His hair blew with impossible wind. Lightning surged in his palms. "Get the kids to safety," he told Nagato, voice more resonant than before.

Before Jett could protest, Nagato had scooped him in his arms with Honor and Horace and was running for the exit. Voltage accumulated around Mr. Thorne until he was immersed in an electric-blue web of lightning. Jett stared on, paralyzed with misery, as Mr. Throne unleashed shockwaves at the tannin's snout with more vengeance than a solar storm. The tannin writhed, screamed, juddered its sinuous head as Mr. Thorne torpedoed the lightning into the lake. Waves exploded. Wind erupted with the force of a hurricane as the tannin went rigid, convulsed, and swung its head before dropping. Mr. Thorne's rage kept accumulating. With a horrid scream, he detonated a sphere of electrosorcery so fierce it was concussing as Nagato punched open the exit and barreled outside into the mountain's belly.

14. THE HIGH EAST

Jett's heart was heavy as a safe as he ran toward the mountain's edge. His lip quivered, but it was Honor who wept, "Toko..." she muttered, running, "I th-thought tannin were figments of legend..."

Behind them, Mr. Thorne shouldered through the wrought-iron exit. Jett, Horace, Honor, and Nagato arrived at the edge of the Sasqis, turned, and watched Mr. Thorne approach. He looked dreary, lost in a dwam.

Minutes passed. No one said a word.

"Poor Toko—" Honor dabbed a fat tear with her sleeve "—I can't believe she's gone."

Jett didn't know what to say. A brisk wind rose.

"Terrible," said Nagato. "After all she sacrificed."

Horace sniffled. "Tracking down Rinona Hollygrew. Trying to find Riley. Trying to fix Pararealm and make things right."

"We mustn't linger," Mr. Thorne instructed. "It's time to end the Umbra's rapacity."

A plank-bridge stretched across a trench toward rocky, carob cliffs, covered in yellow smog. The sky overhead was pale with chiffon clouds. Nagato gripped the bridge's roped handles and stepped onto a plank. "One at a time, shall we?" He tip-toed across. Honor went next, then Jett, Horace, and Mr. Thorne. "The Spurned Cliffs are secluded but not abandoned," Nagato warned on the other side. "If a crag moves or the ground shifts..."

"Asag?" asked Honor.

"Behemothic rock toads," Nagato confirmed. "With large appetites."

The jagged track cut through steep tors and knotted karsts. For the remainder of the day, the party endured, sweeping their eyes about constantly and pausing whenever loose rock kicked up and trundled down slopes. At diverging routes, Mr. Thorne would rise, crane his neck, then gander back with a scowl and press forward without word.

"My feet are blistered," Horace complained later. "My socks are full of blood. And it's hot." He stripped off his saber-tooth tiger overcoat. "Can't we ditch these? I'm burning alive."

"If you desire freezing to death on the way home, go ahead," snorted Nagato. "Now quit your insolence."

"Store them in your packs," Mr. Thorne suggested, but didn't do the same.

In a quiet alcove at dusk, the party set up camp.

"Nagato, what became of the Greymarch Army?" Jett asked, munching blood-sausage.

"Whispers were that fexts and revenants scattered to the edges of the world. Other beasts slipped into dark crevices and disappeared in the skies. But most were slain."

"Did you ever personally confront the Gulog?"

"The Baron of the High East, Greatest of the Liches, Leader of the Greymarch Army," Nagato repeated from memory. "Thankfully, I did not. The Gulog was leading an assault on the Holtmoor when I made way to Umbra Castle."

Jett slept dreamlessly that night, mourning Toko dearly. Nagato, Mr. Thorne, and even Honor traded watch. Horace provided no further blunderings.

*****

Jett felt like he had barely closed his eyes when Mr. Thorne woke him. The party packed quickly under the steel blue and tangerine moons and hastened northeast. By mid-morning, stunted, gnarled trees began to appear as they arrived at the end of the Spurned Cliffs, demarcated by a vast overlook. Nagato set a finger to the lips and led the party closer.

"We now sit in the belly of the beast," Nagato uttered. Wracks of charcoal clouds hung above buckled Dead Valley, replete with sludge-streaked peats and jagged, black canyon slopes around it. At the valley's end was a lake of magma with a fortified bridge vaulting up to an inselberg. Black lightning cut suddenly across the horizon. Jett's eyes followed it up the inselberg to the splintering black spike constructed on it, Umbra Castle. Her battlements were stacked indelibly over each other like organ pipes. Yet, it looked destitute, with shingles missing from the belfries.

Horace gestured to bridge rising over the magma. "We're supposed to cross Caroten Lake via that without being noticed?"

"Like I explained on the Isle—" Nagato pointed far away at clumps of thick, mangled vines which covered the eastern face of the inselberg "—we climb."

Horace reeled back. "Are you crazy!"

Nagato stared out, contemplating. "Strange. Dead Valley was brimming with thousands of the Greymarch Army when I was here last. Thorne, you're sure Uma reclaimed her fortress?"

"She has to be here."

Jett couldn't help but notice Mr. Thorne was reluctant to reply.

Nagato drew his kusarigama blades. "We move at my pace. We must proceed with haste." He shrouded the party in shadow, then tore along an eastern ridge with them down a macilent track bestrewn with encampments long vacant and bone long decayed.

"Strange," Nagato repeated as they arrived at the inselberg's wall of vines. He scanned the ebon sky. "The High East feels completely deserted." He crouched. "Jett, Horace, jump on my back. Honor, you're on Thorne's."

"What if you fall?" Horace asked, glancing at Jett for support.

"Stay if you want," Nagato said. "If it was me, I wouldn't worry about the climb though. My concern would be the colossus oaf-guards roaming atop the inselberg."

Jett wasn't fond of either option. He hopped on Nagato's shoulder. Horace compiled.

"Trick is to not look down." Nagato pulled them onto the lowest rung of the fishnet vine and began to ascend with ease, testing each notch before committing. The wind rose the higher they ventured, and Jett's hands began to sweat voraciously. "Almost there," Nagato said halfway, straining.

Jett glanced down accidentally. Breath fled him. He gripped Nagato tighter. Horace was wincing. "Horace, what is it?"

"I've got to pee!"

"Pee on me, kid, and I'll slice it off!" Nagato roared. "Ready your windguns. We're almost done."

Nagato pulled them onto the inselberg. Jett and Horace leapt off and drew their windguns. Nagato flexed his blades, but no colossus oaf-guards were in sight and the inner gate to Caroten Lake was fastened shut at the start of a pleached road with leafless trees. Mr. Thorne and Honor arrived, and the party rushed to the nearest tower across the cobbled ground.

"Be right back." Nagato scaled the stone tower agilely and snuck into a window high above.

"Seems to know his way around," said Horace.

"This is wrong," said Jett.

"Something's amiss, I agree," said Mr. Thorne.

The wooden door at the tower base unlocked and opened, and out poked Nagato. "Coast is clear. Remain leery."

Horace theatrically tip-toed that way.

"Not like that!" Nagato yanked him inside, giving Jett much needed cheer; that is, until he entered Umbra Castle. Inside was glacial. Not cold like the Sasqis; no, the cold was more of a hollowness, a permeating lack of hope. "If Uma is here," Nagato said. "I expect she'll be in the rearmost tower."

"Reckon that's the highest one?" Horace asked.

Nagato rolled his eyes.

"I don't understand this," Honor said.

The party swept across the bottom level of Umbra Castle, easing around walls and catching glimpses of ghoulish shrines and cobwebbed pianos, once magisterial. Staircase windows provided views of Dead Valley below, no less intimidating from another vantage. The party heard nothing in the second tower stack. Same in the third and fourth. The steps became steeper and more uneven. At last, Jett noticed a flicker of light emanating on the highest landing, which put him on alert. A buttressed door, wrapped in iron chains and a padlock, stood before the final chamber. *Why's it locked?* he wondered.

Nagato sliced the padlock and ripped the chains. The party charged inside.

"Hasn't my rest been disrupted enough..."

They were in an incredible den with crystal chandeliers, palatial rugs, pelage sofas, but no fireplace. A pallid woman was staring at the wasteland behind Umbra Castle. She had knotted, sable hair and was wearing a blood-stained ivory dress.

"Uma," Mr. Thorne called out. "Your corruption and deceit ends now. Surrender, and you will see your day in court. Otherwise prepare to die!"

Uma turned. Her needlelike face was leprous and crystalline. Her haunted eyes roved over the party. "Empty threats carry no weight, Norman." She glided over. Her feet drifted above the stone.

"She's a... a..." stammered Horace.

"Banshee." Mr. Thorne was stunned.

Uma floated to Horace. A vein pulsed in her diaphanous neck. "What's wrong-g-g, pumpkin? Never seen a ghost before?"

Horace trembled, said nothing.

"And you." Uma floated toward Nagato. "Shadow Bender. How dare you step foot in my family's castle. How did the Iconoclasts bring you back to life?"

"*Your* family?" Mr. Thorne shouted. "You bewitched my father! Because of you he was put to death. My mother's world was shattered. Because of you she spent the rest of her days a shut-in."

"So much spite spawned from so many lies..." Uma thrust her hands over her see-through heart. "Your father was the most wonderful man I'd ever met. He loved me, and I loved him, on our own volition."

"You lie!" Mr. Thorne screamed.

"Gene married your mother for stability," Uma thundered. "But he loved *me*. Oh, your father was brilliant. Handsome and generous. All we wanted was to live in peace."

"In peace?" Honor burst. "Then why murder Ruth Schrödinger?"

Uma turned toward the windows. "A tragic accident. Ruth's demise was never our intent. I revived the Gulog necromantically to get to Earth... I'm ashamed of what transpired after."

"Don't believe her," Nagato warned.

Jett stepped closer. "But *why* visit Earth?"

Uma's dead eyes focused on him. He felt like she was reading his mind.

"A half-century ago, on a rainy night with a super-blood moon, an Earthling named Gustave Domingo arrived by mistake on Gene's farmstead. He and I were there on a romantic getaway. We fetched Gustave from the estate. He was loony, wrecked off sorcererspice, rambling incoherently about an object called the Tetrahedron hidden in the stairwell beneath Earth. Domingo claimed that the Tetrahedron *extends time*, and that the stairwell entrance was below La Nouvelle-Orléans." Uma glanced at a watercolor portrait of Gene above the mantel. "We wanted to spend eternity together. We became obsessed with the idea of obtaining the device. Before Gene and I could extract more, the sorcererspice in Domingo's body dissolved and he teleported back to Earth. Gene and I collaborated for years thereafter, hoping Domingo might reappear and that he hadn't already found it. Gene and I foraged through Pararealm's oldest archives for remedies or conjurings before resolving to use Ruth and her remarkable ability."

"You tricked her?" Honor realized.

"Gene paid her a tremendous sum to mend the quantum barrier to Earth, under the guise of research. Took the better part of a decade. By then, Gene and I were too old to make the journey ourselves, so, we elected to send a capable, unyielding servant to retrieve the Tetrahedron for us. Ruth opened the quantum barrier at my grandfather's cabin in Redroot Forest that fateful evening. When she saw the Gulog with us, she tried desperately to shut it." Uma shuddered. "The Gulog murdered her then Gene forced it through right as the quantum barrier closed."

A chill crawled over Jett. The Gulog had worn a brilliant, midnight gem embedded in a gold locket on Halloween. *It was wearing the Tetrahedron*, he surmised.

"Gene made me flee once news of Ruth leaked," Uma continued. "My heart broke into a thousand pieces when I learned, remotely, of his death. I had no will to go on..."

"So you killed yourself," said Nagato, void of remorse.

Uma surveyed the party, distraught, and nodded. Her haunted eyes then spotted the ifrit horn. She eyed a mount on the wall with an identical brother horn, then stared back at Jett. "My grandfather gifted me that. General Zoon stole it. GIVE IT BACK."

Mr. Thorne marched forward. "General Zoon?"

"*He's* controlling Governor Ness." Uma fluttered closer. "Zoon and his sister discovered mine and Gene's plan somehow. *They* kidnapped Riley and forced her to try and reopen the quantum barrier to Earth. But she couldn't. She was just a girl."

"What happened to her?" Jett demanded, growing irate.

"I don't know, truly. But the sheep-goat audit is all a façade to identify another Quantum Manipulator, so I assume the Zoons ditched her." Uma stretched out a translucent hand. "My ifrit horn!"

Jett's stomach wrenched at the thought of a kidnapped and discarded Riley.

"How did the Zoons revive your spirit?" Nagato asked.

"Galen! Brewed a necrophilic potion. Gargaunts come weekly and force it down my

210

throat. They can touch souls, unlike people. It's traumatizing."

"That two-faced hunchback!" Mr. Thorne growled. "I'll kill him!"

"My ifrit horn," Uma roared again.

"So the Zoons want the Tetrahedron," Honor said, thinking aloud. "But why pass so many strict laws and imprison innocents?"

"I don't know," answered Uma. "But be wary of them, particularly him."

Nagato flashed his eyes dangerously at Uma. "What d'you mean?"

"General Zoon's a *parasite*. He absorbs the physiologies and abilities of those he eats. And somehow he fed on something with dermal hide. I heard Mesmer mention it once." She again motioned at the ifrit horn. "Give it to me! I've been more than fair."

"Don't trust her," Nagato repeated.

"I loved your father," Uma said, "with all my heart."

Mr. Thorne nodded at Jett. He unslung the ifrit horn, walked to the mount, and planted it in.

"How about we walk across the bridge this time?" Horace said, heading for the door.

Uma drifted to the pair of ifrit horns and began muttering in a nefarious dialect.

Nagato stiffened. "Uma. Stop!"

"What's she saying?" gasped Jett.

Uma's focus was unbroken.

"The stairs," Nagato urged. "Now!"

The ifrit horns glowed.

15. DYEUS TOWER

Uma glided back from the wall mount as the ifrit horns dislodged and hovered over the open floor. "Time to play, my pet." She rubbed her hands together as a cavernous shadow formed under the ifrit horns and, from the underworld, out climbed a hooved minotaur. Its waist was wrapped with a belt of skulls and in its hand was a threaded bull whip. The horns lowered and fastened on the ifrit's head. Uma swept before it and muttered in the foul dialect again. The party crashed through the door. Mr. Thorne sent shockwaves over his shoulder, blasting stone as the ifrit charged and smashed through the rubble, snorting rabidly. Its massive arms battered the walls and shook the battlement.

"*Oh man*," Horace shouted.

"Damnit, Thorne," Nagato scorned. "I told you. Emotion is a weakness!"

The party leapt down the staircase and sprinted toward the other side of the next landing. "Oh man," Horace shouted again. "I don't think we're gonna make it!"

"Shut up Horace!" Honor snapped.

"I don't think we're gonna—"

"Nagato?" Jett turned, still running, for Nagato had stopped and widened his stance. "Nagato? What are you doing? Come on!"

The party paused at the end of the landing as the ifrit emerged down the stairwell. It tramped toward Nagato, howled with the force of a cyclone, and cracked its whip.

"He's lost his mind," Horace cried.

Clenching his kusarigama blades, Nagato sprung forward, and sliced the ifrit's chest; the whip barely missed. The ifrit wailed and lashed at Nagato, connecting this time. Nagato flew back, a yoroi sleeve torn with a nasty gash underneath. He hopped to his feet. The ifrit cracked its bull whip in the air as Nagato's kusarigamas surged with black energy. He stormed forward.

His right blade punctured the ifrit's ribs. His left bore into its thigh. He leapt over the beast and hammered both blades in its clavicles. The ifrit howled in horrendous agony as Nagato jumped higher. His blades sliced through the ifrit's neck, decapitating it and sending midnight-blue blood oozing everywhere. The ifrit's head fell from its hulking body and jumbled across the ground, horns clanking as the body toppled over like an earthquake, boom.

The party stood in idle astonishment as Nagato strolled over, ifrit blood dripping from his blades, and casually cracked his neck. "I suggest we proceed."

"Holy cow," Jett exclaimed.

"That was amazing," Horace cheered.

"What about Uma?" Honor asked.

"We need excorelixir to vanquish a banshee. Excorelixir we don't have." Mr. Thorne sent shockwaves above the staircase, cratering the passage, then turned toward the next staircase and began walking, consternating, "Dermal hide. I don't know of any rhodium daggers left, Nagato. Nor another weapon which can pierce that armor."

"There is a blacksmith who can forge any blade," Nagato explained. "Though I don't know if she remains."

"Remains?" said Horace.

"Her name is Nori." Nagato glanced at Mr. Thorne. "Of Dyeus Tower. She sits with Reinhold the Convoker in the clouds."

"*The* Dyeus Tower?" Honor asked. "Isn't that—"

"In the Periphery." Nagato nodded, steadfast.

"The Periphery is unmapped territory. My parascouter will be useless," said Mr. Thorne. "You know the way?"

"The warrior who trained my father embarked to Dyeus Tower eons back. I don't know the route, but I'm confident it's reachable."

The party exited Umbra Castle and headed for the bridge. Nagato sliced the latches inside the gate. The drawbridge clanked down and they headed across fiery Caroten Lake.

"Friends of the Umbras are not welcome in these lands any longer!"

Down in Dead Valley, a brawny woman was perched atop a striped golden-white, magnificent canine with a fluffy tail. She had vine-like raven hair and a spiked javelin.

"A warlock," said Nagato. "Shall I kill her?"

"What is it with boys and violence?" Honor cupped her hands around her mouth. "We are the Umbras' *enemies*. We mean you no harm."

"We can't be sure," Nagato countered.

"I'm Chieftress Chasseur of the Zodiac Tribe. My people see to it the High East may never again be reclaimed for evil deeds. Prove you're not an ally of the Umbras."

"Self-appointed guardians against evil, yet you've failed to notice the Zoons," called Mr. Thorne. "Or a banshee." He motioned toward the highest turret. "Uma summoned an ifrit which attacked us. Our intent was to end her conspiracy. But we were deceived."

With a worried look, the warlock lowered her javelin.

Mr. Thorne placed a hand on his chest. "I am Norman Thorne. Beside me stands the great Shadow Bender of legend, Nagato. The young trio have all been afflicted by the Zoons. We are going to Focal City to stop them."

"I'm Farrah." The warlock rubbed the canine's neck. "And this is Raiju, the thunder dog."

Raiju woofed and wagged his tail. The party roamed down the bridge. Magma bubbled and popped under them.

"Wassup, Raiju?" Jett said, petting the thunder dog's fluffy mane. "Nice coat. You look hungry." Raiju licked Jett's face with his wet, bristly tongue.

"You're wounded," Farrah told Nagato. "The ifrit?"

"Nagato wrecked the beast!" Horace complimented, then reconsidered. "I suppose that's been our only victory..."

"Then I'm sure you could use a proper meal and a good night's sleep. Please, join me in our commune." Farrah clicked her tongue, spurring Raiju to kneel on his bandy legs. The party took saddle, and, with a heaping bark, the thunder dog ripped across Dead Valley.

"The Zodiacs are outcasts," Horace whispered to Jett. "I'm not sure we should trust her."

"Hush." Honor jabbed Horace in the back.

"Ow. What'd I do?"

At the edge of the Spurned Cliffs, Raiju veered onto a concealed, arid pass which rounded the tract. In the distance, a behemothic boulder pivoted and hopped to another crag. Jett's eyes brightened as the rock-toad hopped. "An Asag." The ground quaked as the asag landed and saltated again.

The wracks of charcoal clouds faded, then the Spurned Cliffs themselves. Early moons rose low in the lavender sky of the Zodiac Desert, an endless vista of lumpy mounds of espresso sand. Jett pulled his tunic over his nose and squinted as sand kicked up and Raiju raced along. Rocking in the thunder dog's cadence, exhausted from the ordeals, Jett dozed off.

***

Raiju's huge belly expanded and contracted with each breath. Jett stirred beside Horace and Honor, both sound asleep against Raiju's belly. The dual moons were high. The sky was mauve and velvet. Jett surveyed around him.

Mr. Thorne and Nagato were standing outside the largest of a field of sand-domes, whispering deliberately. Jett ambled over. Raiju stretched luxuriously and yawned.

"The Zodiacs have convened. They are determining what to do with our request for aid in the Periphery but refused to let us elaborate our urgency."

"Thorne and I are mulling over our next play," Nagato added. "Like whether we should—"

A spattering of mumbles came from inside the central sand-dome. Farrah emerged, looking pleased. "We have adjourned after an impartial session. I've permission to take you to the Periphery tomorrow. I'm afraid we've no knowledge of Dyeus Tower's whereabouts, however. Your best bet resides with the half-life Brody, who exists in the ether." She glanced at Jett. "In exchange, we require your windguns."

"How about our saber-tooth tiger overcoats?" Jett proposed.

"No." Farrah set two fingers in her mouth and whistled. Raiju sprung to his feet and galloped over, tongue flopping, causing Honor and Horace's heads to drop in the sand.

"Oi, what gives?" Horace barked, cleaning his hair.

"Seriously," Honor agreed. "I was dreaming of Cape Nautic. Lowell and I were walking along the wharf to a blithely summer sunset..."

"Ha!" Horace cackled. "How lame."

Farrah smirked. "Follow me."

She escorted the party through the vista of sand domes. Raiju gamboled beside them (nearly as big as a dome himself), occasionally sinking his front paws in the sand to wait for Jett to play before leaping up and prancing away.

"You know Horace, the Zodiacs are nomads," Farrah said. "Just because we aren't integrated in society, that doesn't make us criminals."

Horace looked to Jett with disbelief. "How'd she hear me?"

"You said it pretty loud."

Horace scratched his neck. "Right. Err, didn't mean to offend you, Farrah. I was repeating what I heard..."

"How did you wind up in the desert?" Jett asked politely.

"A group of Pararealmians believed further conflict was inevitable after Prince Icarus took the throne," she explained. "Our ancestors favored peace over the bustle of city life, so they dislocated from society in a risk-averse kind of hope."

"So you're hippies?" said Horace.

Nagato chuckled.

"The Zodiacs have endured these sands for many moons. The remoteness has shaped us in different ways. We are obedient to the natural order of the world and feel we are more in touch with the blessings of the Karmabird. Label it as you'd like." Farrah unlatched a cozy dome. The party filtered inside and Raiju barked goodnight.

***

The party departed the Zodiac commune with replenished packs and Farrah and Raiju in the morning. The desert dipped, climbed, and shifted as Raiju galloped across the dunes. Gradually, the landscape began flattening. The sand thinned, and Jett began to notice white tile underneath. At the tip of the sand, Raiju skidded to a halt, and Jett stared into a white abyss.

"It's... nothing," he muttered.

"That's the Periphery," said Farrah.

The party dismounted. Farrah passed Mr. Thorne a burlap pouch. "Place these sand-opals behind you. Form a trail. When the pouch is empty, make camp, and wait."

"Then what?" Horace asked.

"Brody will come in time."

"How encouraging," Nagato grunted.

Farrah scowled and swung her vine-like hair. "I warn you: don't stray from the sand-opals, or you may be condemned to wander the Periphery for eternity." She rubbed behind Raiju's ear. "We'll return every dusk. Farewell. Keep faith." With a wave from Raiju, the duo blazed away.

"So..." Horace grumbled. "To beat General Zoon, we're trekking into unmapped territory to search for a windsurfer... to get directions to a place no one knows how to get to?"

"Sounds about right," said Jett, equally as unsure.

Mr. Thorne stuck his nose in the pouch and pulled out a pyramid-shaped, burgundy stone. "Looks like we've maybe got a hundred. Doubt we'll get too far."

The party faced the abyss and voyaged in. Their shadows stayed behind.

"Let's say Brody arrives and knows how to get to Dyeus Tower," Jett theorized. "How do we get there without leaving our sand-opal trail?"

"A conversation we'll have with him," Mr. Thorne said.

"There's another major presumption we're forgetting," said Honor. "We're trusting Uma. What if General Zoon doesn't have dermal hide? What if the Zoons never visited her? Or what if they did and she's biding time to warn them?"

"Nagato and I deliberated this intensely," Mr. Thorne acknowledged. "We all operate with incomplete information in life. Probabilistically, we should forge ahead. The risk of facing General Zoon without a rhodium dagger supersedes relying on Uma's word." He planted a sand opal on the indistinct ground.

"I'm scared," Honor said.

"As am I," Mr. Thorne replied.

"Mr. Thorne," said Jett. "I've been wondering something. Was Toko more than a friend?"

Mr. Thorne looked inquisitive. "Why do you say that?"

"Your body language since the Sasqis. I've been watching you. Plus the sorrow behind many of your words."

"You're rather shrewd, Jett. I miss Toko with every breath."

"I was always curious why you weren't married and had no kids," Honor admitted. "You and Toko had plans after all this, didn't you?"

Mr. Thorne stared into the structureless horizon. "Yes. But life, as it often does, had other plans."

***

The only measure of time in the Periphery was the rations remaining in the party's packs. Six meals had passed when Jett said, "There isn't wind out here. How does Brody windsurf?"

At the edge of the horizon, an orange-marmalade sail took shape and grew fast. The windboard underneath it weaved. "Yo!" Brody waved. "Marvelous out, right? No chunder all day." Brody had crimped, dirty-blonde locks and sunburnt cheeks. He cut the windboard toward the party. "I know you, little dude?" he asked Jett. "Pretty sure I do."

Jett laughed. "Don't think so. The Zodiacs told us to find you."

Brody doubled back. "Wild. Whatchu bennies up to?"

"We're looking for Dyeus Tower."

Brody looked like his mind backfired. "Cruised the Periphery all my life... seen things, seen a lot of nothing. I do know of a road, but I dunno where it goes."

Honor furrowed her brow. "That doesn't make sense."

"Could you take us?" asked Jett.

"A tow-in? Wull... okay!"

"How would you get us back?" asked Mr. Thorne.

"Read the winds, o'course."

"Brody, you're one-hundred percent confident you can relocate our camp?" Nagato confirmed.

"Yep. So how about it then?" Brody pointed at Horace. "Pudgy, let's ride."

Horace purpled. "What'd you call me?"

"He said you're fat." Nagato pushed Horace forward.

"Get a running jump, pudge," Brody suggested. "I'll handle the rest."

Horace clenched his fists. "If you call me pudgy one more time—"

"Horace," Honor warned. "Mom and Pop."

Horace jogged by the windboard and leapt on. Brody didn't falter as Horace rolled atop and stood. One by one, the party repeated the process.

"Righteous!" Brody cut the windboard into the infinite horizon. "Time to shred."

"How did end up out here?" Jett asked.

"Huh, little grom?"

"How'd you start windboarding?"

"I was born doing it."

"Huh?"

Before Jett could ask for clarification, violet, marbled columns bearing crystal wreathes appeared at the entrance of a violet road which snaked and crisscrossed into oblivion. On each column was a plaque: DYEUS TOWER (this way!).

"You mean it was this close the whole time?" Nagato sibilated. "What a waste of a couple of days!"

"The road looks like it goes on forever," Horace muttered.

"Brody, could you take us to the end?" asked Jett.

"Hmmm... no chunder in sight. Seems fine." Brody sailed onto the violet road.

As they cruised, the party apprised Brody of their quest. The whole time, Brody would interject, "Rad! Gnarly! Wuuu, heavy..." The violet road ceased earlier than Jett anticipated, marked by a giant violet recliner and a snoozing, violet giant (a man a hundred times a normal one). A giant ladder with a giant diving board was propped above a carpeted violet seesaw beside him.

"Mr. Giant," Mr. Thorne greeted. "We seek passage to Dyeus Tower. Is this the right spot?"

The giant snored.

Horace tugged Mr. Thorne's sleeve. "Isn't there a rule about not waking sleeping giants?"

"Hell-o-o-o?" Honor called as Brody cut the windboard in a circle.

"Stop sleeping!" Nagato jumped off and strutted over.

"Nagato, I'm telling you," Horace warned. "Waking a sleeping giant is a bad omen."

Nagato reached as high as he could and poked the giant's ankle. "Wake up, oaf!"

The giant didn't.

"Tickle his feet," Jett said.

Nagato crossed his arms. "No way."

"Do it," Horace shouted.

Nagato huffed and tickled the giant's hairy underfoot. The giant giggled in a deep baritone. Nagato kept tickling. "Hehe." The giant giggled, dreaming. "Hehe. Hehe." The giant shook to and took a gander around him. "Hey! Wow. I haven't had visitors in... I don't know. Need a lift to Dyeus Tower?" He pushed himself up, nearly squashing Nagato. "Oh, hey, Brody."

Brody stared back, incredulous.

The giant looked amused, his gorilla arms hanging idly. "You don't remember me?"

A light dawned in Brody's airy mind. "Oslo, bro-o-o. How's it hangin'?"

"Oh, you know." Oslo shrugged and refocused on the party. "You have payment, I suppose?"

"There's a remittance?" asked Mr. Thorne.

"Remittance?" Nagato barked. "Quit using those kind of words."

Oslo beamed. "The payment isn't for me." He shrugged again. "Guess you can sort it out up top. How 'bout... ladies first?" He beckoned Honor to the lowered end of the seesaw and headed for the ladder.

Honor fidgeted. "What do I do?"

Horace nudged her. "Sit. Duhhh."

Honor shuffled forward, sat on the seesaw, and glanced at Jett as Oslo bounced on the diving board. "One." He bounced higher. "A'two. A'three!" He cannon-balled on the seesaw, propelling Honor upward with so much velocity she was gone in a blink.

"Goodness..." Jett, Horace, and Brody muttered.

"Who's next?" Oslo cheered, resetting the seesaw.

"See ya, Brody!" Jett went forward.

Brody gave a thumbs-up. "Fly, little grom. Fly high, high, high."

Oslo jumped and Jett spring-boarded up, soaring through indistinct white sky past pastel-yellow clouds into a pink horizon. The two suns reappeared the higher he went, along with a floating, porcelain hemisphere with gardens, pools, and a palace. Honor was standing on the floating hemisphere with a sloth-like man. "Don't worry," she called as Jett sailed past her. "The cloud'll catch you!"

"The what?" Jett's momentum stopped. He began falling. "AHHH!"

The sloth-man yanked a lever. A puffy cloud materialized at the hemisphere's edge. Jett plopped onto the fluffy, cloud pillow. Astonished, he crawled off.

"Kind of fun, huh?" Honor chuckled.

"I'll say."

The sloth-man reset the lever. The cloud dematerialized.

"Meet Djinn."

"How do you do?" Djinn droned.

Horace came zooming through the pink clouds. "No, no, no, no, no!"

Nagato trailed Mr. Thorne. Once the party had arrived, Djinn placed his arms behind his back and led them toward the palace. "My praise for reaching us. It's not often we've visitors. If I may... what brings you here?"

"We seek a rhodium dagger," said Jett.

"To save the world," added Horace.

Djinn's eyebrows raised. "Is that so."

Inside the gleaming palace were two giant thrones the size of Oslo's recliner. In them were two giants the size of Oslo: an athletic, celadon-colored woman with a spiked mohawk and gold hoop earrings; and a bean-bag-shaped, fuscia-colored man with two antennae and eyes so thin they looked closed.

"Nori the Blacksmith, Reinhold the Convoker," Djinn announced. "Your talents are requested."

"Satisfy us then," Reinhold, the bean-bag-shaped man, commanded.

"Yes... the remittance," Nori added.

Mr. Thorne eyed Nagato.

"Well," said Djinn.

"Well what?" Horace asked.

"Your joke."

"A joke?" said Nagato.

The party glanced at each other, miffed, surprised.

"Anyone confident?"

Honor stepped forward and cleared her throat. "Nori, Reinhold, how do astronomers organize a party?" Neither moved. "They planet." Honor stood at attention, awaiting laughter, but Nori and Reinhold's faces were cement.

"Stupendous effort, Honor." Horace shoved her aside and inhaled. "There's a fine line between a numerator and a denominator. But only a fraction of people will get it!" Reinhold groaned. Nori turned away. Honor stuck out her tongue.

"Nagato?" said Mr. Thorne.

"Nope."

Jett racked his mind, moved closer. "Did you know that if you're running from a serial killer, you're both running for your life?"

Nori rubbed her chin. "Both running for your life..."

Reinhold's mouth opened, closed.

"Running for your life..."

Nori slapped her knee. Great chortles filled the palace from Reinhold. Djinn joined in the laughter, his cheeks reddening with glee.

"So," Nori said, settling, "what is it you're after?"

"There is a grave threat in Focal City," said Mr. Thorne. "The conspirator has dermal hide."

"I see. Rhodium is quite rare," Reinhold surmised. "I am not sure if there is enough left in Pararealm to forge a blade..." He waddled down from his throne.

Nori dexterously hopped from hers as Djinn snatched a diminutive vase. The entire group sauntered outside. Reinhold took the vase, waddled far away to an actual bean bag beside a circular fountain and sat, cross-legged. Nori and Djinn led the party toward a beatific garden on the other side of the hemisphere.

"What's he doing?" Honor asked Djinn.

"Harmonizing with Pararealm's rhodium to convoke it. The rarer the resource, the longer the aggregation takes."

"Great," said Horace.

"Nori?" Jett said. "If we're in the Periphery... what's beyond it?"

"The Wall of Light, certainly." Nori gave a placid nod. "Impassable in this life."

The suns had lowered when a swirling tide of metallic particles flew across the horizon. The particles swarmed, in a vortex, over Dyeus Tower then settled nicely in the vase by Reinhold.

"Ahh." Djinn strolled over and escorted Reinhold back.

"Will this be enough?" Reinhold asked Nori.

Nori snatched the vase and stalked into the palace. Sharp clanking sounds soon arose. Jett imagined molten rhodium mending into a scintillating dagger.

Nori reemerged later with one arm behind her. "I present... your rhodium dagger." She endowed Nagato with a serrated, whitish-silver blade with a hilt of celadon and fuscia stone.

"We can't thank you enough." Nagato slid the rhodium dagger in his yoroi.

Reinhold rubbed his belly. "Time for mud tea." He doddered into the palace.

"And I a good sweat—" Nori bounced onto a lawn and began martial art kicks.

"They get preoccupied," Djinn said.

"So—" Nagato clapped "—where's the path down?"

"There isn't one." Djinn blinked.

"*What*?"

"There, there. I can take you anywhere you wish."

Nagato stomped. "Why'd you have to phrase it like that? Are you saying you can teleport?"

Djinn blinked again. "O'course."

"I was so distracted with finding Dyeus Tower," Jett stressed. "I haven't even thought about how we'll get to Focal City and get everyone to safety." His positivity leaked away.

"What d'you think Thorne and I have been doing while you slept?" Nagato said.

"It won't be easy, but Nagato and I have something up our sleeve." Mr. Thorne turned to Djinn. "If you will... take us to Samedi Bridge."

16. FOCAL CITY

Jett set his hand on Djinn's shoulder, along with the rest of the party. In a flash, Djinn and the party were standing in the bed of a shallow creek below a shabby bridge. The suns were setting. "Good luck," Djinn said, and, with a *POOF*, he disappeared.

"Where are we going?" Honor pressed.

Mr. Thorne walked toward the bridge. "How often have you been to Focal City?"

"Hardly ever. Pop isn't fond of it."

"Understandable. There's a theatre that's been rundown for years. Rumor says it's haunted. This merely serves to keep folks at bay." Mr. Thorne approached a steel door under Samedi Bridge. "I know this because of Toko. Her family is divided, you see. Half belongs to a clan of bandits who smuggle contraband around Pararealm. Turnbull Theatre is one of their secret avenues in and out of Focal City. The Iconoclasts made a deal to use their routes in exchange for protection via the Intelligence Service."

"You allied with thieves?" asked Jett.

"Sometimes, one must side with a lesser enemy." Mr. Thorne wrested the door open and flicked on a light. The gloomy arcade lit dimly. "I assure you it's safe. Help lies at the end."

"How?" Horace pried.

"Mindlink, Horace. Fenton Warbler and I have been in contact."

The party exited through a grandfather clock in the backstage of Turnbull Theatre, which was teeming with dusty costumes and old props that reminded Jett of Shakespearian plays. Mr. Thorne crossed the untidy floor and parted the curtain, then steered the party through to the auditorium, up the aisle and out to the concession area with a decommissioned popcorn machine. A figure lingered.

"Fenton?" Mr. Thorne whispered in the darkness.

A parascouter light flicked on.

"Turn that off," Mr. Thorne ordered, the light briefly illuminating Fenton's foxlike face before darkening. "How are we?"

Fenton glanced outside at the pristine, empty street. "Focal City's unsafe. Governor Ness has enforced a curfew in all Pararealm's major cities. Even our most loyal allies have begun skiving their responsibilities." He inspected the party. "I was sorry to learn of Toko. She was a compassionate person."

"Any news of our parents?" Honor asked.

Fenton sighed. "I've little to tell you. We did ascertain that Governor Ness's dungeons are not below Fuzz Precinct like we believed," he said, mainly to Mr. Thorne. "The dungeons are below PsyMart Headquarters. It is likely the Hanes are there."

Mr. Thorne was rattled. "You didn't reveal this before."

"The intel is fresh."

"Doesn't your family own PsyMart?" Jett verified.

"We lease space in the stores. PsyMart is, by charter, a part of the government."

"What came of the Isle?" Horace probed.

"There were casualties on each side. Some Iconoclasts escaped. Most were taken to the dungeons, including Reese." Fenton again casted his eyes into the shaded streets. "The Fuzz have been raiding homes without cause, hunting us." Fenton and the party headed for the side door, then scurried through alleys under the cover of Nagato's shadow. Focal City was more magisterial than Enopolis, Jett gathered. The causeways were lined with grand, ivory-strewn manors, courtly governmental offices, and an ornamented clocktower.

Fenton fumbled with his keys at the rear of his brownstone.

"I didn't share something," Mr. Thorne told Fenton. "It's not Governor Ness we're after. It's Mesmer and General Zoon. Galen too."

Fenton stopped cold. "The Zoons?"

"They revived Uma Umbra's ghost."

"We must free the prisoners," said Nagato. "Then we dismantle the Zoon network prior to a direct assault on the General and Mesmer."

Fenton opened the back door. Bob and Buzz Fuzz, plus a horde of other Fuzz officers, were huddled in the parlor looking spiteful. "Freeze!" ordered Bob. "All of you. Hands up."

Mr. Thorne stared at Fenton wrathfully. "I... relied on you... revealed secrets. How could you do this to me, to our mission?"

"The Governor took Fiona and my children..." Fenton whimpered. "They came with caustic cannons..."

"Interesting insight into your nerve!" growled Nagato. "There's your traitor, Thorne!"

"HANDS UP," Buzz commanded.

Mr. Thorne unleashed a torrent of electrosorcery into the parlor as Nagato bent the shadows around the party and fled. "*Directions*," Nagato said.

"Left!" Mr. Thorne gasped, then "Right!" at the next turn.

"We can't go to your estate," Honor instructed. "Where are you taking us?"

A city-wide siren wailed suddenly, accompanied with the voice of Captain Fuzz. "People of Focal City, people of Focal City, a dangerous group of Iconoclast fugitives has snuck into our city limits. These criminals are extremely depraved and vie to flout our peace. The Fuzz Precinct orders you to stay inside. And a reminder: anyone caught aiding or abetting an Iconoclast will be punished to the severest extent. Rest assured: Governor Ness will keep you and your families safe!" The speaker crackled. The unsullied streets flooded with more and more Fuzz officers.

"Left there. Then the next block," Mr. Thorne directed.

"This is madness!" Horace cried out.

Jett was panting and sweaty by the time the party stopped at a mechanical freight door of a warehouse. Mr. Thorne punched numbers into a keypad. The freight door rose. The party funneled in. Mr. Thorne clamped the door and locked it.

The warehouse was lined with towering shelves of assorted supplies, boxes, and industrial equipment. "A Thorne Corp. storage facility?" Honor observed. "We can't stay here."

"We only need a few minutes." Mr. Thorne ran his hands through his hair. "I thought I knew Fenton... that spineless wimp."

"Governor Ness took his family," Honor stressed. "You mustn't be pitiless."

"We've all lost something!"

"Save your compassion, Honor," Nagato hissed. "Character is measured in the most trying situations."

Jett stepped between everyone. "What are we *doing*? All of Focal City is after us. The Fuzz could tear through these doors any minute."

"We aren't staying," Nagato affirmed.

"So what's our plan?"

"Ness will be at the Governor's Mansion, correct?" Nagato asked.

"His agents may already be evacuating him." Mr. Thorne paced about the industrial aisle. "Unwise for us to make any assumptions."

The party went quiet, everyone ruminating.

"I have a suggestion," Nagato said wryly after a stretch. "But it will require award-winning acting on Honor's part."

She tensed. "Why do I feel like I'm not going to like this?"

***

Ensconced in Nagato's shadow, Jett, Horace, and Mr. Thorne trailed Honor, who was visible out front and had resentfully used her mimetic ability to change into a milk delivery girl. Mr. Thorne had provided her a basket of corked, glass milk bottles from his storage facility.

"I can't believe you convinced her to do this," Horace chuckled to Nagato.

"Quiet," he snarled for the fiftieth time on the quest.

Sirens still wailed across Focal City. On the next street was an imposing consulate with a shingled, forest-green roof and squat belltowers. "Fuzz Precinct," Mr. Thorne whispered to Jett. "Not somewhere we want to be."

Around the corner, the prodigious, pearl-white Governor's Mansion was hunkered behind a white brick wall. Fuzz officers surrounded the perimeter, most near a central gate.

"That one over there. At the southern wall," Nagato directed Honor.

She skipped toward the lonely officer standing uselessly to the side. Her basket swung. The bottles clanked. She hummed and caught the officer's eye.

"Hey, *you*. Are you deaf? You can't be outside with 'em Iconoclasts run'n 'round."

"But *you* are," Honor pointed out, the basket coming to rest.

"I'm *allowed* to be," the officer scorned. "I'm the authority in Focal City."

Honor scowled. "Shouldn't you be chasing the fugitives then? I guess you got demoted."

The officer hoisted up his belt, defensive, and pointed at his chest. "I've an important job here. I'm tasked with keeping Governor Ness safe."

Honor glanced down to the guard post. "Seems like *they've* that duty."

"Why you—"

"On the mention of duty, *I've* an urgent delivery for Governor Ness. He needs his nighttime milk, right away."

The officer scratched his head. "But Governor Ness isn't here?"

"He isn't?" Honor raised the basket and examined the bottles. "Oh, no. His milk will curdle! Where do I take it then? Hurry."

The officer squinted. "Maybe I ought to speak with the guard post."

Honor leaned forward and sniffed. "Ew. You stink."

"What!" The officer raised his arms up and smelled his armpits. "No I don't. Must be the sewer line."

Honor pinched her nose. "I think you're just accustomed to your B.O. If I was you, I'd run home and shower." The officer blushed. Honor waved the basket. "I'll be out of your hair as you tell me where to take this delivery."

"Baba's Bathhouse," the officer snapped and turned his back.

"Perfect." Honor skipped away.

The party convened in an alley.

"Honor, you were brilliant." Jett beamed. "Really."

"Wow, you think?"

"And you look grea-t-t," Horace laughed.

"Ugh, you ruin everything." Honor restored her tunic and dropped the milk basket.

"I know Baba's," Mr. Thorne announced. "Many heavyweights frequent it."

"Then by all means... lead the way," Nagato demanded.

The party snuck in shadow toward Baba's amidst the lockdown. Sirens rang. Patrols swept Focal City like mice searching for cheese. Thrice the party paused as Fuzz officers passed. In time they made it to a backstreet across an inconspicuous shop with an unlit sign: BABA'S. Standing under it were four muscular agents from The Governor's Office with caustic cannons. Mr. Thorne nodded to Nagato, then took the trio behind a row of trashcans and crouched.

"Best you not watch," Mr. Thorne told the trio as Nagato bolted over.

Crisp sounds of kusarigama blades slicing through flesh came, plus strangled shrieks. Nagato returned, his yoroi sprinkled in fresh blood, then escorted the party across the street. Jett was sick of the carnage that Nagato so easily shrugged away.

"We're closed—" Baba's clerk said, not looking up from her magazine when the door opened. Mr. Thorne zapped her unconscious.

Five steaming pools were dispersed across the candlelit bathhouse. A buxom woman with cyan hair tied high over her head lingered in one with hairy Governor Ness, who had a bowl-cut and gold necklace. Jett stood transfixed, for the woman was topless and Governor Ness's mouth was on her nipple. "What the..." he and Horace chorused.

Mr. Thorne charged. "Mesmer! Out of the water. Your charade is over!"

Governor Ness let Mesmer's jiggly breast fall. He wiped his lips, looking more dazed than Horace on the delicashroom.

"Just who I've been dying to see," Mesmer sneered, eyes like chips of ice. "Come to join the other Iconoclasts in the dungeons, have you?" She patted Governor Ness on the head and reached for a towel.

"Uma revealed everything," Mr. Thorne yelled. "She despises you." He eyed Nagato. "Get Ness. Fast."

All the light in Baba's went out. Splashes came. Shadows spread and the light bounced back on. Nagato, soaking wet, had Governor Ness in a headlock and a kusarigama to his neck. Mr. Thorne sent lightning into the steamy bath. Mesmer stiffened then went limp like the tannin, floating face-down.

"Where... wh-where, where am I?" Governor Ness stammered, scanning the party. "Norman? Is that you?"

"Don't fall for this," Nagato warned.

"You've locked away innocents under your Ordinance of Order," Mr. Thorne barked. "Defiled our democracy. Defaced Pararealm's good name."

Governor Ness pointed at Mesmer's floating body. "Pectukinetics! I was under enchantment via her... mammary glands. I would never—" Governor Ness rubbed his cheeks and whined "—I barely remember how I got here. I barely recall the past year."

"Don't believe him," Nagato repeated and allowed Governor Ness to fall to his knees.

"Norman, please. I'm the victim of Mesmer's controls."

Horace snickered. Honor smacked him. Jett held in his laugh.

"I don't trust him either," Honor said. "He locked up my parents."

"Please," Governor Ness cowered.

"He's culpable, Thorne." Nagato grimaced. "We needn't discuss it more."

"If you want to see the suns rise," Mr. Thorne said. "Take us to the dungeons under PsyMart Headquarters and free your prisoners."

Governor Ness nodded rapidly. "I'm sure the schematics are in my paraketch." He snatched his robe, tied it around his bathing suit, withdrew a watch, clicked through. "Yes, yes. Here. I'll take you."

Mr. Thorne sidled Governor Ness, studied the schematics, then compared them to his parascouter. "Seems there's an unlisted passage in the water canals under Pararealm Power Plant. It's a few blocks away."

"You cross us, your head becomes my souvenir," Nagato threatened as Governor Ness retreated with the party out the back of Baba's. They entered the underground canal through a manhole by a cooling tower at Pararealm Power Plant. A river of wastewater ran in the center of two walkways. Artificial lights lined the subterranean passage. Governor Ness and the party dashed to an iron gate, which Nagato split with his blades.

"We're under PsyMart Headquarters." Governor Ness eyed the paraketch and guided the party as Nagato silenced Fuzz officers. "Around this corridor is the dungeon door." Governor Ness stopped suddenly, leapt back, and planted himself against the wall. "Hold up!" He shoved the party away as a fireball whooshed into the hall.

"What in the blazes is that?" Nagato asked.

Governor Ness bit his fingernails. "It's a—a—a cacodactyl."

Jett stuck his nose out. A furry, hellacious, fire-breathing pterosaur was chained and guarding the dungeon door. The cacodactyl screeched. Smoke furled from its nostrils as it prowled and spit another fireball at the party. Jett jerked back as the fireball passed, nearly singing his eyebrows. Governor Ness's teeth chattered.

"Is there no other way in?" Nagato took the paraketch and studied the schematics. "Blast. Thorne, I'll need you with this."

Mr. Thorne snagged shackles from the wall and latched them on Governor Ness's hands. "Watch him." He nodded to the trio then raced into the chamber with Nagato.

Mr. Thorne's electrosorcery attacks clashed with the cacodactyl's flame, causing incredible surges of bluish-orange energy to explode out the chamber. The cacodactyl screeched. Shadows gathered. Colors combusted. Kaleidoscopic energy waves burst and collapsed.

"How does General Zoon control this thing?" Horace yelped. "Hey. *Hey*. Where is he?"

Governor Ness had morphed into a greyish-glassy mass and was zooming away.

"He's a benzikist," Honor gasped. The greyish-glassy mass gyrated at the bend then evaporated down the next hall. "I bet he's getting General Zoon!"

"Nagato!" Mr. Thorne's voice came as more fire and lightning and shadow clashed. "GET THEM OUT OF HERE!"

Nagato swooped around the corner and dragged the trio away as a spectacular electric blue detonation flooded the underground, leaving silence in its wake.

17. A Twist of Fate

Jett broke free of Nagato's grasp and dashed toward the chamber.

"Stop!" Nagato shouted.

Jett rounded the corner. He froze. The cacodactyl was toppled over Mr. Thorne, both unconscious. The air drained from Jett's lungs as he moved closer and heaved the cacodactyl's great wing off Mr. Thorne. He knelt. Tears amassed in his eyes. "Mr. Thorne. Get up." He tried to stir him. "Alright? Mr. Thorne. *Please.*" His voice cracked with pain. "Please... wake up." Mr. Thorne laid limp, eyes shut behind his cracked, circular glasses. His eggplant topcoat was scorched black.

Nagato, Horace, and Honor arrived. Nagato leaned down and felt Mr. Thorne's pulse.

"Well," Horace muttered.

Nagato surveyed the barred dungeon. "We must release the prisoners." He sprang over and severed the lock.

Jett sniffled. "We can't leave him like this."

"On your feet," Nagato demanded.

Honor pulled Jett up.

Spirit crushed, he followed a despondent Honor and Horace and a determined Nagato into the dungeon, an inverted tower with sub-terranean levels of iron-barred cells. Jett leaned against the rail and peered down. Prisoners had their hands clenched around the bars and were chattering and staring up with fearful eyes.

"Mom?" Honor cried, searching.

"Pop?" Horace yelled out.

"Horace?" said a voice.

"Honor?" said another.

"Mom!" Horace took off down the spiraling walkway.

"Keys," Harlow called. "By the door."

"Never mind that." Nagato careened down the spiraling walkway and sundered the cells, releasing hundreds of shaggy, starved prisoners who scrambled up toward freedom.

In minutes, an exhilarated crowd—Harlow, Hessa, Reese, Panoplía, other Iconoclasts and innocent citizens—had formed near the dungeon exit.

"Jett, the wunderkind! You did it!" Harlow flung his arms around him, then hugged Horace and Honor. Harlow was frail and deprived of sunlight.

"We're not out of this yet," Nagato said.

The excitement stopped. Rejoice vanished.

"What d'you mean?" asked Reese.

"General Zoon, Governor Ness... many enemies remain at large. We must get to safety and devise a plan. We're behind."

"Where are Norman and Toko?"

In a doldrum, Nagato led the Iconoclasts toward the cacodactyl. Gasps rose.

"Toko perished as well," Honor said, eyes red.

Reese stooped near Mr. Thorne. "Always stubborn," he lamented, a tear leaking. "You always had to be the hero."

Harlow nodded. "He was exemplary."

Two Iconoclasts lifted Mr. Thorne. The crowd proceeded through the underground back to the main water canal.

"*Vermin*! Get back in your cages." General Zoon was planted in the running waterway. He looked reptilian up close, face like a death adder, and wore a mustard-yellow military cape. A pale, malnourished teen with gangly hair was trapped in his claws. Governor Ness was flanked by their side in his robe, snickering.

"Riley!" Reese shrieked.

Jett was speechless. He half-understood what he was seeing.

"Dad!" she pleaded.

General Zoon cackled. "I smell guilt, Reese. How much pity must you feel for your daughter... never being able to find her, to save her from me."

"You soulless bastard!"

Governor Ness squealed with delight. "You heard the General. Back in your cages."

"Or what?" Horace growled.

General Zoon smirked. "Or I'll eat your bones, boy... after I gnaw through Riley's." His claws compressed around her shoulders. She winced. "Do not think any of you will escape this." He noticed Mr. Thorne's limp body. "I see my slippery friend Norman is one step ahead. A shame. I had hoped to torture him for the death of Mesmer."

"Riley's your only hope of reopening the quantum barrier to Earth," Honor bellowed. "You wouldn't dare hurt her."

"Don't talk about what you don't understand, girl." General Zoon spit with rage. "I WILL RULE PARAREALM WITH OR WITHOUT HER. With or without the Tetrahedron. You know nothing of what you say."

"So that's it?" Harlow gasped. "All you're after is power? Driven by mere greed? Envy?"

"Silly, Harlow," General Zoon promulgated and waved a finger. "My secrets will not be unlocked so easily."

Reese moved closer, an outstretched arm trembling. "General, please don't hurt my daughter anymore. We can resolve this. We can find a way forward... perhaps a treaty."

General Zoon cackled again. His laughter penetrated hope. "Admirable sentiments, Reese, but you fail to understand that all of you belong to me. You're my pets, zero ground to stand on." His claws bore further in Riley. She let out a plangent scream. "You people are so... weak... so encumbered by petty attachment. It's sickening."

"This isn't a game," Hessa shouted. "This is reality. These are peoples' lives you so readily disgrace and throw away."

General Zoon licked his lips. "Mmmm. Guess you'd better stop me."

Nagato unfurled his kusarigama blades, keeping the rhodium dagger hidden in his yoroi. "Any imp can kidnap a child. Let Riley go and fight me at full strength. I want to see what all you've been feeding on, parasite."

"So. You know a bit about me?" General Zoon thrust Riley into Governor Ness' hairy arms. "I've fed on many things, most recently my prisoners. Misery is wonderful sustenance. Very well, great Shadow Bender, how I wished we'd meet once I learned it was you the Iconoclasts resurrected at the Isle." His mouth curled. "Prepare yourself. Death is my specialty. And I love serving it."

Nagato widened his stance and flexed. "As do I."

General Zoon stretched and flounced in the water, but paused. "Oh, I almost forgot. I only transform if someone counts me down."

"You're kidding..." Nagato groused.

"Not in the slightest. Come, now. Manners must be observed."

"Five, four, three, two, one," Nagato hissed. "Happy?"

"Elated." The waterway cracked under General Zoon's feet as his body quadrupled and he morphed into a hulking crocodile with ridged, mustard-yellow dermal hide and black freckles. His eyes sloped toward his ginormous snout and a violent, pink energy encapsulated him. "I'm gorgeous, don't you think?" he snorted.

Face blooming with rage, Nagato strutted into the waterway and bent the shadows so that the canal went pitch black.

"You can't hide from me, warrior," General Zoon chortled. "I can... *smell you*. I can... taste your flesh on my tongue. I can... hear the blood course in your veins."

"Tear him to pieces, General," Governor Ness cheered.

"Before I end you, warrior, I'm going to make you an offer," General Zoon rumbled in the dark waterway. "You have great potential. We both know it. Under me, you could be a god. Pledge your loyalty and have Pararealm's riches at your fingertips." The crisp sound of Nagato's kusarigama blades came. A beam of pink energy exploded from General Zoon's snout. He swept it across the main, crumbling the infrastructure, deepening the waterway. "So valiant," General Zoon snarled. "So obstinate. You refuse to accept your own fate!"

A wail came.

A groan.

A horrific splintering.

A skin-crawling shriek.

"Devour him!" Governor Ness clapped.

Standing in the Iconoclast crowd, Jett's blood boiled. He leapt into the canal.

"No!" Harlow reached out as Jett plunged into the shadows.

"Power is all that matters," General Zoon shrilled in the shadows. Nagato puled like a wounded dog. "Everything else is a delusion... a worthless fantasy."

Jett splashed toward the sound of General Zoon's chewing. And from the bottommost pit in his stomach, a ferocious force grew. Bluish-white fusion immersed him and an energized ball of light grew in his palms. "Take this, YOU FREAK!" With that superhuman scream, he sent the fusion ball into General Zoon's chest, propelling him backward. General Zoon dropped Nagato into the running water. The shadows released. The canal brightened. Jett blasted more fusion balls into General Zoon as Nagato rolled over and whipped a kusarigama blade at Governor Ness, who vaporized to avoid being beheaded.

"*Riley.*" Nagato threw her the rhodium dagger with all his might.

She caught it and sprinted to Jett's side. "Keep him pinned!" She bounded ahead and—with a heaping, two-handed thrust—impaled General Zoon's head. General Zoon flopped over with a dire moan. His pink energy dissolved. Riley, panting, slowly turned and said, "NO. WAIT!"

A terrible sting erupted in Jett's ribcage.

Governor Ness had stabbed him with a karambit blade. "Eye for an eye, kid," Governor Ness grinned, vaporized, and flew away.

Sputtering, blood filling his lungs, Jett glanced at the mutilated body of General Zoon then at Nagato's appalled face as he plummeted into the water.

18. The Halo

Golden light shined all around Jett. Golden light radiated within him. The golden light was him. Weightless and infinite, Jett felt total peace.

"I've have been observing you," a voice lilted. "You've shown courage and sacrifice, ruth and integrity during your stay. For this reason, I give you the choice of returning to your friends and, ultimately, your family. Is that what you wish?"

Jett thought, yes, and in his bodiless state, he floated through the golden ether and, slowly, Pararealm came into view. He woke, lying on his back, heart twanging, staring up at a regal, prismatic bird with vermillion, gold, and white hackles. Black stripes ran down its wings and neck, and a golden halo surrounded it. The Iconoclasts, and a swelling crowd, had circled in amazement outside PsyMart Headquarters. Jett sat up.

"You helped save Pararealm," the Karmabird said telepathically. "I endow you with the Cumu Cloud so that you alone may travel back and forth from Earth. Simply whistle, and the Cumo Cloud will appear. But I ask that, just this once, you return through the quantum barrier so that Riley may shut it for good." With a majestic hoot, the Karmabird fluttered its dazzling wings and lifted off the ground, leaving a trail of golden energy in its path. Jett and the crowd remained motionless as the Karmabird sailed toward the suns, and the deep sorrow hanging over the day morphed into abundant sense of faith.

"What did the Karmabird tell you?" Horace asked, ecstatic, helping Jett to his feet.

Jett rubbed his ribcage. The wound from Governor Ness was gone. "She thanked me, and offered passage home." He glanced around. "Where's the Governor? How's Riley, Nagato—"

"Easy," Reese assured. "All will be fine. We'll catch Governor Ness in time, along with every vile person who aided him, including his allies in the I.S. and all of Fuzz Precinct."

A tear shimmered in Honor's eye. "We couldn't save Nagato. The damage done by General Zoon was irrecoverable." The Iconoclasts bowed their heads. "I had grown to truly care for him. Twice he saved our world without praise."

A feeling of divine connectedness ran through Jett. "I think Nagato chose everlasting rest. I can't explain it, but I think he elected to be with his long-lost family. I think the Karmabird offered Nagato the same choice."

"Thankfully—" Hessa grinned "—our prized electrosorcerer will recuperate in a matter of days. Norman's energy drained fighting the cacodactyl. His body entered a state of severe shock, but he did not die."

"Nagato and Toko will be remembered in an immutable way," said Reese. "We owe them everything. As we do you, Jett, more than we can ever repay."

"Others deserve credit!" he exclaimed. "Magnus Rime in Zegna Town, Farrah the Chasseur in the Zodiac Desert, Doris Gibbons in Dowse Town—"

"Too right you are." Reese smiled. "All of Pararealm will come together over this victory."

Jett focused on Hessa and Harlow, feeling chipper. "I've got to admit, I wasn't sure I'd ever see you again. So many things went wrong on our quest."

"So we heard." Harlow held his wife.

"Riley ought to have the quantum barrier mended in no time," Reese explained. "Then we can get you back to Earth and your true family."

Jett caught Riley's eye. She looked like a worn-down machine, destabilized. "I can't imagine what you endured. And for so long."

"What the Zoons did was sickening," Hessa agreed.

"I don't reme-member m-much from the e-early years." Reese slung a strong arm around his daughter, as she replied, "Only a sense of y-yearning. A missing of love and w-warmth. The Zoons kept me in a c-cellar in En-nopolis, forced me to p-progress the abilities I inherited from my m-mom. Later, they took me to a basement in an old house in Redroot F-forest and installed teleblockers to prevent escape." She shuddered. "I couldn't mend the quantum barrier no matter how h-h-hard I tried. General Zoon and Mesmer were outraged, intolerable of my m-mistakes. Then, maybe two years ago, they began c-consulting somebody in the High East. Mesmer in particular was irate that the consultant knew so little and devised the Order of O-ordinance. Around then, I at last was able to start m-mending the b-barrier, albeit w-weakly. Finally... one day... I opened it, and someone crossed over." She stared at Jett. "You."

"You were there?" he said, a pang of remorse emerging. "You saw me leave Horn House."

"Through a tiny, begrimed window in the basement. I wondered who you were. The weeks after, I lived vicariously through you; rather, my imagination of what you were up to. Seeing you provided strength. I felt the tides had changed."

"Why did Bob and Buzz Fuzz visit Horn House, though?"

"Happenstance," presumed Riley. "I assume they stumbled on some paperwork and had a look. They noticed the cellar door, tried lazily to get in, but gave up because The Zoons put a metalock on it. Those idiots could have saved me."

"Addle-brained," said Horace.

"I don't think anyone besides the Zoons themselves knew the real plan," Riley continued.

"And the ifrit horn in the dresser?" said Honor.

"Ifrit horn?" Riley's face morphed with concentration as if reliving many scenes. "The Zoons gave me many dark artifacts which they believed could enhance my ability. I was brought an ifrit horn maybe a year back."

"But how did the Zoons travel from Focal City to Horn House to the High East without anyone noticing?" Honor burst. "And how did Mesmer first put Governor Ness under pectuk-inetics, and did Governor Ness like being kept under her spell or was he corrupt before that? And did the Zoons identify another Quantum Manipulator among us? And—"

"Honor," said Horace. "You're going to det-onate. Let it go."

"The Zoons had you open barriers inside Pararealm," Jett realized. "That's how General and Mesmer Zoon traveled around."

Riley nodded with admiration. "Intraworld barriers aren't so hard."

"Come on," Reese told Riley and Jett. "Let's get you both cleaned and rested."

Horace smiled ear-to-ear. "And a meal at Goosefeather!"

***

Over the ensuing days, the party's entire quest was documented in detail—from the battle at the Isle of Iconoclasts through the journey over and under the Sasqi Mountains to Umbra Castle in the High East to their arrival in Focal City—plus all the happenings beforehand collecting the parastones, the Iconoclasts inception by Mr. Thorne and Reese, locating Rinona Hollygrew, and the full truth of the Gulog and the murder of Ruth Schrödinger. Jett's hand was wrung with merriment and his back slapped thousands of times as visitors from all over—Odin Stine, Doris Gibbons, the Dhampirs, Rory the Reconnoiter, Clarence Cleese (who brought an enormous bundle of chocolate treats) and even the Rimes—converged on Focal City to celebrate the freeing of the prisoners and the renewed democracy. Erstwhile, the benevolent faction of the Intelligence Service and civilian authorities shut down the Fuzz Precinct, raided the infected divisions of the I.S., arrested Galen in his grotto, Fenton Warbler in his townhome, and captured Governor Ness in the Southern Shrublands, then fed Uma Umbra's spirit excorelixir, ending her spectral existence and stifling the terrible ordeal spearheaded by the Zoons.

Thereafter, a splendid ceremony occurred in Enopolis in which Nagato, Toko, and all those who had met their demise or suffered under the Zoons' tyrannic reign were honored. Approaching sundown on the third day, the Iconoclasts—including a rejuvenated and exultant Norman

Thorne—accompanied Jett and Horace on the Silver Pigeon to Horn House to see Jett off and to seal the quantum barrier permanently.

"How're you feeling?" Harlow gave Jett a big hug in Horn House's entry.

"I guess, alright." He shrugged, genuinely unsure, flooded with so many emotions.

Harlow thinly grinned. "Give your parents our best."

"He can't tell his parents about this," Hessa reminded. "They'll think he's a lunatic."

"Oh, right." Harlow scratched his head. "Well, you know what I mean."

Horace sighed.

"What's wrong?" Jett asked.

"It's just... I figure we won't see each other much."

"You think after all this I *won't* visit? Earth's gonna be a bore! I've got to hone my powers anyhow." He hugged Horace then turned to Honor, who blushed. "Honor, it's been a—"

"Pleasure." She pecked him on the cheek. "Something to remember me by." She backed away with twinkling eyes.

Jett went ruby-red.

"See, Horace," Reese said. "Even more reason for Jett to visit!"

Mr. Thorne crouched. "I know Nagato was supposed to be the big, bad warrior in all this... but in my mind, you're as much of a fighter as he was. You have such promise ahead, Jett. I look forward to seeing you again."

Jett grinned and hugged Mr. Thorne. "I've been thinking," he muttered as they released. "Someone should visit Nagato's homeland and tell his people how kind and caring he was. He deserved that."

Mr. Thorne nodded. "I've been thinking the same. Well worth a trip to Asija Village."

A thought sprung in Jett's mind. "And then what?"

Mr. Thorne's head cocked.

"Now that this is over, the Iconoclasts will disband, right? What will you do?"

"I'm not sure. I feel a bit feeble. Perhaps take post at Sooth Institute. A part of me has always wanted to teach. Good news—I've plenty of time to figure it out. You look after yourself now."

Jett turned toward the closet, where Riley stood. "I'm with Horace," she said. "You better return to Pararealm *a lot*. Don't make me reopen the quantum barrier and come get you."

Jett laughed. "You won't have to."

"Well. Ready then?"

"I suppose." Jett spun once more and surveyed the crowd—the Hane family, Mr. Thorne, Reese, all the Iconoclasts and friends—and wondered how much time had passed back in New Orleans. A tear sprouted in Hessa's eye as she lovingly shooed him on. He turned and slowly, steadily, the closet morphed into a phantasmal portal and a fly buzzed under the door. The closet ripped open with such force that the door slammed against the wall! The Gulog burst through with a brilliant, midnight gem in a gold locket hanging from its neck. It gaped at the crowd with its depraved, sinewy face. "At laaassst," it crooned, curling a wiry hand and adjusting the saggy, pointed cap. "I'mmm baaa-cckkk!"

Reese rushed forward, dual-bladed axes of hardened light forming in each hand. "Gulog! Baron of the High East, Greatest of the Liches, Leader of the Greymarch Army, murderer of my wife, I hereby command you to die!" He charged.

Mr. Thorne shoved Jett through the closet and tossed the door shut as Reese and the Gulog clashed. "Riley, SEAL THE BARRIER." Electric-blue shockwaves burst under the frame as Mr. Thorne joined Reese in battle. Jett grabbed the handle from inside and yanked wildly, but it had become inoperable.

"MR. THORNE. RILEY," he cried. "LET ME HELP YOU!"

"WE'LL BE FINE. I PROMISE," Mr. Thorne called as the light under the door dimmed then disappeared entirely, along with the noise.

Hating the situation, subsumed in darkness, Jett lowered onto his stomach and crawled the opposite direction. Soon, another strip of light appeared. He crawled toward it, then out from under his bed, and stood in his room. It was just after sunrise. A tepid breeze rustled his curtains. The window was open. Had the Gulog crawled under his bed and waited for the quantum barrier to reopen? Jett went to shut it, thinking, as a creak came.

"Oh—you're up." His dad opened the door to his bedroom with a steaming cup of coffee. "Just checking on you. You know... to make sure no vodun monster nobbled you last night." He winked, took a sip, checked his watch. "You've got an hour before breakfast. That wacko Cooper is gone and was dejected. Seems Detective Dreyfus was right."

Jett fought a smile. His dad closed the door and moseyed back down the hall, whistling.

Whistle, Jett remembered. He turned back to the window, set two fingers in his mouth, and blew loudly. A pinkish-yellow cloud manifested just beyond the sill, ready to take him for a majestic, paranormal ride.

Printed in Great Britain
by Amazon